TRY NOT TO DIE

Escaping the Cult

ANGEL VAN ATTA

MARK TULLIUS

VINCERE
P R E S S

Published by Vincere Press
65 Pine Ave., Ste 806
Long Beach, CA 90802

Printed in the United States of America
First Edition

ISBN: 9781961740334

Cover by Jun Ares

I dedicate this book to all of you, my wonderful readers. You are what keeps me going back to the metaphorical pen. You give my characters life within your minds, and without you they would just be scribbles on a page. You are my superheroes, and I appreciate you, always.

Angel

Thank you to Angel and all the authors who have allowed me to try not to die in their worlds.

Mark

A Note from the Publisher

Every collaboration in the *Try Not to Die* series offers a unique experience. Sometimes I develop the story, other times I focus solely on crafting the death scenes, and occasionally, like in this case, my contribution is primarily in refining the language. This incredible tale was brought to life by Angel, and I'm truly grateful to have been part of her creative journey. We hope you have a thrilling experience. Good luck—and try not to die.

And be sure to check out the flash fiction piece at the end of the book which I wrote for a giveaway winner.

Mark Tullius

TRY NOT TO DIE

ESCAPING THE CULT

"Hurry!" Ma says, grabbing up Little Joe and putting her hand out to me.

Pa's at the front door, talking to someone in a loud voice. "What would he want with our Ruby? She's a simple, plain girl. We've always done what's been expected of us. We've already given one child. No more. No more." Pa is almost yelling and begging at the same time. He's a big man, Pa is, and people listen when he talks, so for him to be pleading like this fills me with dread.

"Please, Joseph, step aside. Father Gabriel sent us himself," the voice says, all soft and gentle-like but also a little cold. "He only wants what's best for us. We're all his children, and he leads us with great wisdom."

I want to stay and listen, but Ma grabs my hand and pulls me to the back door of our tiny kitchen.

"Great wisdom?" Pa scoffs, his voice even louder than before. Anger fills those words of his. "Was it great wisdom that got our Sammie taken away and put in a cell at the bottom of that ugly damned house? Wisdom that keeps us from even seeing him?"

"Joseph, Samuel was caught with paraphernalia. A cell phone, no less," says a new voice, one I recognize. One most Children of Gabriel would. It is Uncle Rayson, a man you could not say no to. Uncle Rayson is a Hand of Gabriel, and he punishes those Gabriel deems in need.

"But—"

"And because of him, fear was spread that caused a Chosen Daughter to flee and live with the damned." Uncle Rayson speaks right over Pa. "We lost an innocent babe to that fear. A child who will now not be saved."

Ma opens the door with her other arm still around Little Joe, holding him to her while he looks at me, scared. She drops my hand and tells me, "Go, Ruby, now! Pa's not gonna be able to keep them distracted much longer, and if you don't run now, you may not get another chance. We saw what they did to that poor girl. We don't want that for you. *I* don't want that for you." Her voice fills with the same terror flooding Little Joe's wide eyes.

I stand at the open doorway, knowing I have to make a choice: stay...or run into the dark night and find my way to the city. Find my way to someone who can help me like *she* was helped. To escape like *she* did.

Katie was Sammie's best friend since we were all kids. Ma always hoped they'd be a match someday, and I think Sammie wished for that too. Heck, we all did. But after Sammie brought that phone in and started showing Katie those videos the outsiders our age were making, something in her changed. She no longer wanted our simple life, the one we've always known, the one we've been groomed for. Instead, Katie dreamed of more. She wanted to go out into the world and be her own self. Make her own choices. Live her own life.

So, Katie tried to run, over and over again, and every time, she was punished. Each consequence worse than the last. Finally, when she came of age and failed one too many tries at getting free, they took her tongue straight from her mouth, they did.

Ma and Pa were in the room, tasked to hold her down. The pain echoed in poor Katie's eyes and in her screams when her tongue was stretched out and Father Gabriel cut the wicked thing straight from her mouth. Wicked because she had used it against us. Katie had told someone she thought could help her, who had ended up just being an Elder from a different sect.

They took her into the Big House and gave her a room, chained her to a bed. It is supposed to be the best role a woman in our *family* can ever achieve—bringing forth the babes of the highest-ranked among us. But us girls whisper to each other about how horrible it would be. To leave the homes we were born in, just to be made to have their children until we're all used up and sent away to be maids. Scrubbing floors and dusting away the cobwebs of the higher-ups when we can no longer bear their littles.

Katie was chained so she could not try to escape again. Chosen only for her beauty she was, but it was her perseverance I admired most. Because she didn't give up. And eventually, she *did* escape. Her belly was swollen with an Elder's child when she ran, but this time, she made it. This time, she was free.

Most of us aren't deemed worthy to be put up in the Big House. We're matched off and allowed to live in our tiny homes, do the jobs we're given, and make families of our own. That's the life we *want* to lead, even if we don't go around admitting it. It would be a betrayal of words to tell anyone this, but we all know it's true. We all hope for it. Everyone is all relieved when what we see looking back at us in the mirror isn't as beautiful as what Katie was.

Is, I guess.

"Go," Ma says again. "Run!"

If I do as Ma says, I will be leaving them both at the mercy of Uncle Rayson. And he isn't a man known for showing any. He enjoys the suffering of others because he says torment is what's best for them. Uncle Rayson preaches it is the only way to redemption. The more pain someone goes through at his hands, the closer it brings them toward salvation.

If I run out this door and down the path into the woods, I have a chance to escape whatever consequence I must pay for Sammie's phone. The phone he showed to Katie, which filled her mind with the joyous evils of the outside world. Which tainted her against the words of Father Gabriel. Which tainted her against *us*.

But if I do that, my parents will surely be punished in my stead. And worse so than whatever it is the Elders have in store for me. They will be made examples of, to ward off any other parents who may wish to smuggle their daughters away.

For we have all heard the whispering since Katie's escape. The fear is like a disease, and it is spreading fast. Folks don't want their daughters to be treated so. They don't want their daughters to lose their tongues or be chained to beds.

So, should I run, or should I stay?

*****

Run! Turn to page 5.

Go with the Elders. Turn to page 29.

I've grown up in a world where we're taught to listen to our parents. They know what's best for us so we should always comply. Guilt at the thought of leaving fills my heart, but if it's what Ma wants, then I must do it. For Ma surely knows better than I do.

I take Ma and Little Joe into my arms and hug them tight, finding comfort in Ma's tight, one-armed embrace. The tears running down her cheeks wet my own. I kiss Little Joe on top of his head and run out the door, into the dark of night.

Our home butts up against the woods, which I know as well as the back of my own hand. They were my childhood playground, and my brother's, too. We spent hours there, with Katie and our other friends, taking turns hiding, seeking, climbing, and just lying around on our backs watching the clouds drift by through the trees.

My feet pound down the path they helped cut through the undergrowth and I run as fast as I possibly can, away from the only home I've ever known, toward a future I can't even imagine. I just need to make it out before they come. Before they catch me.

I run and run and run until I'm at the line we've never dared cross. It's marked by an almost imperceptible boundary made up of trees grown densely together and underbrush that's not been trampled by the feet of playing kids. None of us have dared to pass, because we've all been taught the stories of what happens in the woods beyond. The creatures living within that darker forest would feast upon our flesh just for daring to venture in.

I stop to catch my breath, leaning against the rough bark of a huge pine, wondering if all those stories we heard and told as kids were true.

Then I hear them coming.

Uncle Rayson and his men, calling out. Urging me to stop and come back before my parents' lives are taken. Before my little brother is forced to go instead of me.

As I stand here looking into that thick underbrush, fear washes over me. I can't let them take Little Joe. My younger brother who can't sleep if Ma doesn't leave a candle burning on his windowsill. The poor little boy who wakes up screaming for her nearly every night since Sammie was taken from us, his dreams filled with terrible monsters. So I do the only thing I can, and I turn back, calling out where I am.

The shadows all around me grow and darken, puddling where I stand. My feet grow cold and my breath puffs out even though the night started out warm when I fled my kitchen door. As the blackness from the shadows creeps up my body, it feels as if I'm turning into ice everywhere the shadows touch.

"Help! I'm over here! Please! You have to help me!" I scream, hating that I'm hoping my captors can save me.

But the shadows are too fast and my body freezes beneath them. I want to scream again, but I can't because my lungs are stuck and I'm numb everywhere.

There's a crackling sound, way down by my feet, of ice moving up my body. The shadows are freezing me solid. And the ice I'm becoming crumbles under the weight of me. My neck's stiff, my mouth stuck open in a soundless scream, as I tip forward. My mind grows cold, my body tilting to the ground to shatter into a million billion pieces.

*****

The correct answer was to go with the Elders. Turn to page 29.

I drag my brother down the path to the left when one of the large bat things swoops down. There's a soft whistling of wind before we throw ourselves forward. The demon grabs at our backs, barely missing my brother's robe as we hit the ground.

The demon screams in anger, the sound so loud and shrill that stalactites shake, some crumbling and falling, crashing all around us. I get to my feet and pull Sammie's arm, urging him on as three more of the evil creatures come for us. The first one comes again, its jaws snapping, great wings blowing a horrible wind that nearly knocks Sammie down again.

I lift up a large stone that had been shaken from the ceiling. I heave it full force at the demon as its teeth scrape at Sammie's neck, a red line appearing as a thin layer of his skin splits. My stone collides with the creature's bony cheek and its eyes grow wide with shock as its head is knocked to the side.

"Run!" I scream, dragging Sammie, stumbling toward the black hole before us.

The other demons grab at us as we approach the mouth of the tunnel. We wrap our hands around the slabs of rough granite that make up the entrance of the cave. The demons land and try to pull us from the rock as we kick at them.

The demon whose skull I caved in gets back to its feet and screams again. The others join its angry call. The sound vibrates the stone beneath our fingers and feet. My teeth shake and it's harder to keep our grasp. Fear creeps in as I thrash my feet harder and faster.

A demon grabs a handful of Sammie's robe in its talons and grunts at us. "Eat!" it says in the darkest voice as it yanks one of Sammie's hands free, pulling him backward.

The one that holds me barks, "Kill!" It threads its shiny black fist into my hair, pulling, bringing me closer to its waiting mouth.

It takes all I have to keep my grip. At the edge of my vision, I see Sammie reach back for the rock, but he's failing, and so am I. We're both about to die. One of the demons lets out a loud shriek of triumph, shaking the entire cavern.

"I'm so sorry," Sammie cries. "This was all my fault. I should never have taken that phone. I should never have showed it to you or to Katie. I should have stayed true."

"No!" I shout, pulling away from the snapping jaws trying to sink its teeth into my neck. "I'm glad we saw. I'm glad she's free and I'm glad I got to try and be free, too." Every single part of me would rather die here in this tunnel with my brother than continue to live my life at the whim of Father Gabriel, or out of fear of Uncle Rayson's fist.

"You're the best sister a brother could ever have," Sammie says, reaching his free hand out for mine.

I let go with one hand and grab his. I lose some ground and see the look of greed in the glowing eyes of the demon holding me. It's all about to be over, but the feeling of calm I get from my brother's hand in mine is worth the seconds lost by letting go.

The demon's cries cause more stalactites to break free. All around us they crash to the ground with great bangs. Just as the demon's teeth are ready to bite my flesh, a jagged tip of a stalactite hits the demon directly between its hunched shoulders, tearing through its body and splitting it in two.

I fall forward and use the momentum to pull Sammie free from another demon's grasp, toward the gaping black hole. We scramble into the darkness of the cave as the two remaining demons jump after us. Their scaly skin makes sandpaper sounds against the stone, but they're too big to fit in past their shoulders, their arms too short to reach us.

We're safe from them. Safe for now. Together we continue on, shuffling deeper into the darkness until the light drifting in around the demons fades. Until we're lost to ourselves. Stuck in a sea of shadow, my eyes useless things that ache as they try to see, but can't.

***

I don't know how long it's been since we've been in here, surrounded by hard rock. At first, we rushed away on our hands and knees because the tunnel wasn't tall enough for us to walk, afraid at any second of some new horror jumping out at us. But after a while, we were so far away we could no longer hear the sound of the demons. So much time passes since the last source of danger that we are lulled into a sense of safety and able to doze. We know we have to hurry because the Elders will know we're missing soon, but we can't help it. We're exhausted from the fear and from the running.

We begin to crawl ahead again. One hand forward, then a knee, moving as carefully as we can through the darkness. Listening for any sign of whatever tries to kill us next, hoping to stumble out of here for good.

"Remember when we were little," Sammie says, his voice filled with his usual optimism, but pain, as well. He winces every now and again as he puts weight on some part of him that hurts. "When me, you, and Katie would play in the caves out by the baptismal waters of the pond?"

"Yeah, Ma found us in there that last time we went and man, did we get the spanking of our lives!" I laugh, and so does he, the sound of it a beautiful thing. A wonderful thing.

"Boy, was she madder than an old wet hen! Pa too, when he found out. But more than that, I think they were afraid." A sadness creeps into his voice. "Do you remember how, later that night, Ma was crying in her bedroom when we were supposed to be asleep?"

"Yeah." Now that he mentions it, I realize how common that was for her when we were growing up.

Ma was always crying when she thought we couldn't hear. I never understood it back then, but now I do. Now I know it was because she was always afraid. Afraid of losing us on account of some rule we didn't follow. Scared Pa would tell the wrong joke to the wrong people. Afraid Sammie or I would see the wrong thing when we were sneaking around places we weren't supposed to go. Now it all makes sense. Living in this community is about doing the right things, and sometimes that's hard, especially for kids, because there are way more wrong things for us to do than there are right.

Sammie crawls close behind. "Do you remember how it smelled, that last time we were there, inside those caves? That last day Ma pulled us out and made us swear we'd never ever go back?"

I know what he's getting at because I *do* remember, and I smell that same smell now. The smell of decomposing leaves and algae and water that's sat around too long. It's coming from up ahead, blowing in on a soft breeze. I know where we must be, and I get excited, crawling faster. This has to be it. The way out.

"When we get out, is there a way to bring Ma and Pa and Little Joe with us?" I ask. The joy of it all fills me up, and I'm happier than I've ever felt. Lighter somehow. We're almost there. We're almost done!

"I don't know, but maybe we can find help out there. Get someone to come and stop it all. Someone who can get them out?" His voice is filled with the same hope as mine, so we don't notice it at first. The way the ground beneath our hands and knees grows soft and wet. How soon there's a layer of water getting deeper as we go.

"The tunnel's sloping down," I say, the mud beneath my palms turning more slippery, the water getting higher. We can't turn back. The only way is ahead, but the joy I felt a few seconds ago, the hope in our freedom, drains away. I want to cry and hit the walls until my fists are broken and bleeding.

"We gotta be close, Ruby. We'll swim our way through if we need to," Sammie says, sensing my change of mood.

I love him for trying to make me feel better, but not even his cheery tone can ease the darkness seeping into my heart. Darkness that's far darker than the cave. Darkness that eats away at my hope and makes me think maybe we won't make it out of here.

"If we're forced to go under, what happens if we don't find a place to get back up?" I'm crying now. As quietly as I can, I cry, the tears racing down my face and plopping into the deepening water. "What happens if there's no air down there?"

"There will be," Sammie says.

Even though I can't see it, I hear the smile on his face. That small twist of his lips that always got us into so much trouble. Now, it may end up getting us killed. But imagining that grin, the fear is so much less. I smile back, knowing he's right. He has to be. We move forward, and as we do, the cave grows taller, and we're able to stand again.

The water gets deeper with every step. It's cold, and the air blowing from some unseen crevice feels warm in comparison, and smells of outside just as much as it smells of wet and rot, telling us we're going in the right direction. I just hope we don't have to swim. Going under not knowing if we'll be able to come up causes me to shake more than the cold water. If Sammie wasn't right behind me, I would probably stop. I wouldn't be able to go on.

The water's almost too deep to continue. It splashes my face, too close to my nose and mouth, my anxiety spiking every time I breathe some in. With each step forward, the ceiling of the cave lowers, and soon our heads scrape against it. I can't see anything and not knowing how much longer I can go before the water rises above my head drives me mad.

"We're gonna have to go under," I say, my face pointing up because the water's so deep. "Can you swim, do you think?"

"Don't worry about me, Sis. I'm right behind you," Sammie says, squeezing my shoulder.

I'm about ready to take a deep breath and dunk under when something splashes in the water behind us. Something large.

Sammie pushes me. "Go, Ruby! Go!"

I dive under and push off the ground, swimming as fast as I can. Sammie's right behind me, his large hands scooping water and banging into my feet. I just hope his thick wool robe doesn't weigh him down.

There's no telling what splashed into the water behind us. Whether it was one of the demons, something new, or just a giant rock falling down. It doesn't matter. All that matters is the way my chest is on fire.

My shoulders keep hitting the cave ceiling. There's no way to breathe even though it's the only thing that fills my mind. My heart races, my lungs desperate to fill themselves. All I can do is to kick my feet, ignore my growing fear of death, the certainty of it rotting my hope with a green, rancid poison.

Nothing attacks us, but we've killed ourselves. We've raced past the tipping point, too far to turn back. My chest jerks as I fight to keep my last breath inside where it belongs. A weird feeling seeps into my brain and even though I know I can't see anything in this place, my vision grows fuzzy. Then I realize I *can* see. That it's brighter ahead. The color of fire dances in the water.

We're almost there.

The cave leads up and I spy the wavy silver plate of the water's surface where the outside begins. Hope blooms in my heart, even as my lungs scream for air.

My head breaks through and I gasp, while scrambling out of the tunnel. I get to my hands and knees, and dig my palms into the rocky cave floor, taking in breathful after breathful, coughing in between. I turn to Sammie, but he's not there.

I dive back under and spot him stuck by that horrible robe on an outcropping of stone. He's struggling, jerking at it but unable to reach the spot where it's snagged.

I push off against the edge of the tunnel and Sammie looks up, pleading for help. He reaches out and pulls me to where the wool snags on the rocks. I unravel it and yank him free, pushing him toward the opening. Sammie grabs the sides and works his way toward the water's edge.

Sammie lies on the muddy ground, gasping as I crawl past him. His coughing turns to laughter, and I can't help but join him, even though it hurts my whole body.

We're in the opening of a giant cave, lit by dozens of torches, their light glowing with some unnatural magical quality that's beautiful and terrifying all at once, making the shadows seem alive.

"How many times are you gonna save my life today?" Sammie asks after finally getting control of himself.

I give him that same smile he always has for everyone else. "Technically, this is only the first. And I kinda hope you don't need me to pull you out of any more water-filled tunnels."

"Well, you *did* get me out of that cell, and if I had to listen to Mad Martha go on for even one more second, I would have ended things for myself. Because oh my gods."

I know he's joking, but I don't like him saying that. I look away, not wanting to ruin his mood.

Living in this community, one of the only ways out is death by our own hands. It's our biggest sin. Father Gabriel says it's a waste of our life's blood, which could otherwise be spilled in the name of our Fallen Angels. But those who give themselves up as tribute die a public death. We're forced to watch and rejoice in the sacrifice freely given.

First, they're laid on a heavy wooden cross, their wrists and ankles pinned to the wood by long iron nails. Our strongest members pull a thick chain attached to the bottom of the cross and haul it into the air so the tribute is hung upside down, mimicking the man-lord Jesus' death to please our own cruel gods.

Underneath the cross is a pile of dried wood and fuel-soaked coals. Once lit, the fire burns bright and high and we all dance around it to the tribute's pain-filled screams, the smell of their charring flesh a stark reminder of our place in things. We dance not because we want to, but because if we don't do our part, we may find ourselves in the bowels of Uncle Rayson's dungeon. In need of salvation. It's no wonder why so many choose to end it for themselves, even though we're taught that such an ending brings eternal damnation. At least then we may find peace. At least then we may find dignity.

"Sis, look!" Sammie stands, his voice filled with wonder.

I sit up, suddenly anxious. Outside the cave is the great pond where many of our ceremonies, like our baptisms, take place, and surrounding that is the dark forest. The sky peeking through the trees is dark and filled with stars. It feels like an eternity has passed since I was brought to the Big House

"We're almost there," I tell him. "We just have to make it through the woods, like Katie did."

"I don't think it's gonna be that easy."

"Nothing worth having ever is," I say, Ma's words coming out of my mouth. Only they don't bring the comfort I thought they would.

Sammie takes my hand and gives it a squeeze. "The work only gets harder the longer we put it off," he says, repeating Pa's words, but with none of his confidence.

I tighten my grip in his and give him a nod.

We walk to the edge of the cave and look out at the pool. It's a part we've never been to before. They say the clear water is fed by an underground spring, the same one that fills our wells. It's supposed to be the source of the magic that controls this place, that Father Gabriel draws from. It's the reason he hardly ever travels outside our borders. Whenever he does leave, he doesn't go for long.

A trail winds around the pool. To our right it leads to the great stone altar, awaiting its next victim. As for the left, I'm not sure where that leads. Out into the forest after following along the water's edge a while. I'm not sure which way will get us out of here the quickest.

"Righty-tighty or lefty-loosey?" Sammie asks.

"To the right is where they would have taken you, and drugged you, and placed you—" I can't say those horrible words. I can't face the reality of what almost was.

"To the left, we've never been because we never dared to venture toward the pond except when we were made to," Sammie says. "Not since Ma caught us here and Pa gave us that beating of a lifetime."

I'm grateful to hear his voice in this place all the children fear. This place that some children sneak away to, either to play or on a dare. A place that some children never make it home from.

"Well?" I ask. It's time to go. Time to choose.

*****

Righty-Tighty. The way we've been before. The way we know.
Turn to page 16.

Lefty-Loosey. Toward the unknown and whatever scared our parents enough to beat us. Something they had never done before or since. Turn to page 100.

"Righty-tighty it is," I tell Sammie, smiling at him.

He smiles back and we walk toward the altar and the familiar part of the woods beyond. It'll be simple for us to find our way out from there. The woods are like a second home for us given how much time we spent running around in them.

The closer we get to the altar, the faster we go. We're not excited to see it, but we're past it, it'll be a cakewalk to freedom. We run as much as Sammie can, and we actually laugh, we're so giddy to be done. We're almost out. Almost free.

But then we see the stone protruding out of the water. Pale gray, stained with blood from the hundreds who have been murdered over the years. Killed in the name of gods who probably don't even exist. Lives taken for no other reason than the sacrifice had seen too much or not done enough when they were asked. Or because they simply asked for more.

"It's so sad here, in the moonlight, with nobody else around," Sammie says, his voice echoing across the flat and glassy the water.

"It's always sad here," I reply.

"Well now, children. Don't be sad," a voice says, freezing us in place. "This isn't a place for sadness. It's a place to come together and celebrate a gift freely given."

I recognize it at once. And the lies it speaks. Father Gabriel walks up the far side of the path, which leads back to the Big House. The path we'd taken for years during recommitting ceremonies. "And what do we have here, but two more gifts for Those Below. Those to Come."

"No," I say, trying to turn and run and pull Sammie with me, but my body freezes in place. I'm unable to move at all as Father Gabriel slowly approaches us

"Please, just let us go. At least let my sister go," Sammie pleads. The way he stands tells me that he's just as frozen as I am. All the hope and giddiness that bubbled up inside me drain away.

"I will, my child. I'll let you both go. To join *Them* and tend to their wants and needs. But fret not, for there will soon come a day when you will be brought back to us, and you'll walk the earth forever as their servants."

Father Gabriel comes up between us, placing a hand on both our shoulders. He turns us toward the rock, and we step into the water as one. We make our way across its surface, our bare feet padding atop the water. I feel lighter than I've ever felt. I feel numb.

Against our will, Sammie and I climb onto the cold gray slab and lie down next to each other. Shoulder to shoulder, we barely just fit, and as Father Gabriel stands above us, the sky erupts into a thousand colors. Purple swirls into red and blue and green. My mind is lost in its beauty as he raises the silver blade high above his head.

The knife slams into my chest, but there is no pain. My body drifts up into that sea of whirling colors. As I join it, I turn and see my body next to Sammie's. The knife slams into his precious heart. As my mind dissolves into the misty hues of death, I feel peace at last. For the first time in my life, I feel the peace of death, and I'm content.

*****

The correct answer was to turn left toward the unknown.
Turn to page 100.

One of the Brothers opens the door for Uncle Rayson, who slips out of the car and moves toward the stairs. I slide out after him and take off running, which none of them seem to expect since it takes until I'm at the edge of the woods across the lane before I hear them give chase.

"Get her!" Father Gabriel's voice booms.

I'm almost to the trees, and freedom is so close, when a burning hand clamps down on my shoulder and throws me to the ground, knocking the air from me.

I'm so confused. How is Uncle Rayson standing above me, glaring down at me in so much disgust I want to cry?

"What do you want me to do with her?" his cold voice asks as Father Gabriel arrives next to him. Both appear to have moved much faster than they should have physically been able.

Father Gabriel looks at me in silence, considering what to do. "Sometimes the youth needs reminding of their place in things. Sometimes they forget. We've seen it before, and I'm sure we'll see it again." He smiles down at me even as Uncle Rayson continues to sneer.

I find my breath again and suck in great lungfuls of air, hating myself for being so stupid.

"Let's make an example of her. Tear out her heart and we'll both have a little snack," Father Gabriel says as if he's discussing the weather. "We'll string her up on a post right on this spot and march everyone all by tomorrow to see. The crows can do the rest. That should settle things down a bit, at least for a generation or two. Or until the end finally arrives."

Father Gabriel's tone is pleasant the entire time. A wolf's cruel smile blooms across his face, his eyes sparkling with excitement.

"Please, I'm sorry," I say, sitting up and scooting away from them.

Uncle Rayson grabs hold of my hair, his nails scraping my scalp. Blood pours down my face, into my eyes. The world is shown to me through a veil of red as I'm pulled up to my feet.

There's so much pain that I scream out and beat against him, though I know it's no use. I'm kicking out, but no matter how hard my shoes strike him, it's as if he doesn't feel it at all.

He laughs an evil cruel laugh, and Father Gabriel joins in. The other men turn away, with only Brother Paul remaining witness.

I look into Brother Paul's eyes, silently pleading with him to save me. But he turns his back like the others and walks up the long stairs and into the open door of the Big House.

"Don't fret, little one," Uncle Rayson says, as if he's talking to a caught bunny or some small child who's seen something scary. "I'll make it quick, for I'm hungry and I love the way a freshly taken heart tastes, just after it's beat its last."

"I promise I'll be good," I say.

"I don't doubt that one bit," Uncle Rayson says as he slips out a knife. He slides it through my shirt, the tip of it parting my skin. A hot kiss of metal slides between my ribs, pressing ever slowly in.

I shudder as the knife pierces my heart, realizing I'm about to die, the blood no longer pumping toward where it should go. And when the darkness comes and takes the pain away, I'm almost happy. because with the darkness there comes peace and, at least in some way, I have escaped this horrible place.

*****

The correct answer was to stay and see what happens.

Turn to page 50.

I bathe myself and lie back against the white porcelain, the jasmine-scented water soothing my body and mind. I don't know how long I lay, but the bath doesn't cool. And while my muscles calm, I watch the tiny flickering flames dance within the clear glass globes of the lamps.

The only choice I have is to wait until tonight. So, wait I will. When the opportunity arises, I'll find my way to Sammie. And together, we'll escape.

Sister Anne comes to collect me, a soft white housedress in her arms similar to her own. She places it on a wooden bench beside the door, grabs the bath sheet, and holds it out for me. I get carefully to my feet and step out, allowing her to wrap me up in it.

"How did the water stay so warm?" I ask her as I dry off.

"It is one of the many gifts from Father Gabriel," she says as she grabs a brush from the shelf.

"But how does he do it?"

"We do not ask such questions here," she says, her voice hard like metal. "It's blasphemous to do so."

"I'm sorry," I stutter, afraid I've offended her. "I didn't know."

Sister Anne runs the brush through my long brown hair. It's still wet, but the conditioner provided to me has made it softer than it's ever been and the bristles slide through easily. She's gentle as she works, like maybe she's not so upset after all.

"It's not your fault. You weren't taught in the same way we were. You weren't meant to be here," she says, her words hushed. "This must all be so foreign to you. So strange."

"I'll try to do better," I tell her as she places the brush back and retrieves my new clothes. "I'll try to learn it all as fast as I can." I hope I sound like I mean it, even though I'm fully committed to getting out of here as soon as the opportunity arises.

"You'll do fine here." She pulls the silky white fabric over my head as I let the linen bath sheet fall to the white tiled floor. "You were a smart kid, back when we had classes together. Always the teacher's pet."

I slide my arms through the long sleeves. The dress falls down over my shoulders. Sister Anne's smile takes me back to when we were friends playing tag and Ring-Around-the-Rosie, whispering about the boys and giggling over who we may one day be matched with.

She was a good friend before she was chosen. Maybe she'll be a good friend now. Maybe she'll be the friend I need to get out of this place.

"Annie, have—"

"Sister Anne. Please." Her eyes swing to the door and back, a warning for me to follow the rules.

"*Sister* Anne, have you ever wanted to run from here? Like Katie did?"

Her hands are on my shoulders in a blink and her fingers press hard into my thinly covered skin. "Listen to me, I beg of you. Listen well," she whispers so fiercely my heartbeat quickens and fear slides its cold fingers around the muscle. "You never know when they can hear you. When they can see you. You have to watch everything you do. Everything you say." Her words come faster and faster as she speaks. Her eyes shine like they're fueled from some internal heat. "Father Rayson's punishments are cruel, and he likes to punish. It's his greatest joy."

"Sister Anne—"

"Promise me," she talks over me. "Promise me you'll do all you can to please them. To make them happy. For if you don't, he'll come for you in the deepest darkest part of the night and he'll do things to you, Ruby," she whispers so low I can hardly hear her words. "Terrible, painful things."

My mouth opens, but I have no idea what *to* say.

Anne turns and shrugs one of her shoulders free from her dress, revealing a triangle of soft pale skin covered with thick red lines, the scars of a lesson she was forced to learn. But even worse than the whip welts are the oval arcs of tiny, scarred-over circles.

They can only be one thing: bite marks, and they're everywhere. As if Uncle Rayson bit her again and again and again. They had to be deep to scar in such a way. Painful.

"Sister Anne, I'm so sorry." My heart breaks for her. It's hard to find breath. It's like my chest caves in on itself with fear for the both of us. I hate that we've both found ourselves here, stuck in this web of other people's desire. "Why do you stay?" I ask, keeping to a whisper. "Why don't you run, like Katie did? Why don't we both?"

"Sister Katie isn't safe, no matter how far away she gets. They'll find her. Somehow they'll find her and they'll bring her back and they'll make us all watch as they redeem her. Don't you see?" She twists back around, her eyes burning, not just with the reflections of the lamps, but with her need for me to hear. "We could try, but we'd die a thousand different ways before we could. We belong to *them*. We always have. We were born to them. And no matter what we do or where we go, if we did somehow survive to make it past the borders of this family's land, we'd still be doomed."

She stares into my eyes, into my soul, looking like she believes every word she says. She'll be no help to me. She'll never want to leave. Never be brave enough to run. They have broken her, and there's nothing I can say to make her see that we could be free.

With luck and all the right choices, we can be free. I promise myself as I stand barefoot before my broken childhood friend that I will make it out. No matter how many times I have to try, I will be free.

***

Sister Anne leads me to my room, a simple box on the second floor with a single window staring out onto our moonlit woods. She hugs me tight before leaving, whispering a final warning in my ear against trying to slip away. That I would never know when their eyes would be on me. With her departure leaves the warmth she brought with her. A warmth I hadn't even known she carried until it was gone away from me, into the thick darkness of the hall.

The bed is large and covered in a soft hand-sewn quilt, each square telling a little piece of our Family's story. Our past and present and future. Little sewn-together pieces of cloth forming our history and our way through the coming end of things and our new beginning after. Pictures filled with sacrifices and demons rising from fiery pits. Circles of chanting Elders raising their hands to the sky even though our heaven is below our feet. Carefully sewn squares show Father Gabriel's offspring spreading out across the globe for generations. Our entire belief system lay there before me on that bed. A bed I'm afraid to fall asleep in, afraid what I may wake to.

There's no closet here. Just a tiny dresser with three drawers holding a modest assortment of neatly folded clothes identical to what I'm wearing now. On the back of the door hangs a thick white cloak, made for those above the rank I woke up as this morning to wear to religious events. Below the cloak hangs a delicate veil, which a Chosen Daughter uses to cover her face at those same events and community meals.

Besides these few things, the room is bare, and I'm filled with a great sorrow for the life I left behind. Back in the house I grew up in. Back where my few trinkets sit inside a room even smaller than this, but so much bigger in all the ways that matter. A room filled with memories and everything I've ever found important to me. Little keepsakes of a life I'll never have again. Because no matter what happens tonight, I can never go back. I can never be that me that was. Everything has changed. And there is no going back for me now. There is no going back for any of us.

I press myself into the space between the hanging robe and the door. The veil is soft against my ear as I press my head against the rough wood. I listen harder than I ever have.

Footsteps fade as someone walks down the hall. A woman's laughter and hushed words rise from a nearby room.

The seconds turn into minutes that turn into I don't even know how long. I wait until the noises give way to silence, and then I wait some more. And when the only sounds are the creaks from a sleeping house, I make my move, twisting the knob and slipping into the hall as quietly as I can.

My feet are bare against the worn, smooth wood and as soon as I step into the hall, dread seeps into me, as if up from the floorboards. It feels like there's an unseeable mist wrapping dark tendrils around my ankles, tugging them back toward my room. I don't know if it's some trick of this place to keep me where I'm supposed to stay, but it won't stop me. The first step is the hardest, as if the invisible strings are real and have substance to them. But I push forward, and the illusion is shattered.

I hurry down the hall, and then down the stairs, one terrifying step at a time, until I reach the first floor. With each step I expect the wood to creak, alerting those around me that I'm doing something I've been warned against. But my feet make the softest sounds as I work myself back the way I'd come.

There has to be a way down into the basement, but I'm not sure how to find it. This place is like a maze, and it looks different than it did before. As if it's changed in the few short hours since I came through its front door. Another magic designed to keep us in, keep us afraid. But I'm not afraid. If Katie did it, so can I. I just have to keep trying.

I finally reach the entryway and stand before the locked front door. I try the knob. It doesn't twist the slightest beneath my shaking fingers. I turn and press my back against the door.

It's cold. Colder than any wood holding back a wall of snow in the middle of winter. I shiver, but don't step away. I know it's a part of the magic show, too, the one that keeps us all inside. And I refuse to buckle to it. I press myself even harder against it as I consider my choices.

To my right the doorway is dark again, as it was when Father Gabriel had his icy grip on my shoulder. It's a wall of black that my eyes can't penetrate, a sense of unease drifting from it. I don't know where that way goes, maybe somewhere they don't want me to see. Somewhere they don't want me to be. Why else would it seem so foreboding?

Straight ahead is that same long hall Sister Anne took me down to bathe. Closed doors are on either side, as well as the stairwell up to my room. One less choice to be made among all those closed doors. One of them could lead to a stairwell down to the basement. But the rest may lead toward countless other things. Worse things. Terrible things.

And lastly on my left, another wall of shadows so dark it looks impenetrable. As if I could walk over and press my hands against the absence of light and would know the feel of it. The feel of shadows beneath my palms.

Again, there must be some reason Father Gabriel would make it seem so dark, so inaccessible. Is he hiding the path to my brother? Or is it there to keep us safe? To protect us from whatever lies within? I need to make a choice. Which way should I go?

*****

Take the doorway to the right. The path down must be through the house. Turn to page 67.

Make my way down the hall as quietly as I can, peeking behind each door 'til I find a stairwell to the basement.
Turn to page 33.

The wall of shadows to my left looks so real, so completely solid, even though I know it can't be so. This must be the way. Why else would they make it seem so impossible to access?
Turn to page 92.

I'm so overwhelmed with the urge to run that my body chooses for me, refusing to take one more step toward this destiny. I rip my hand free from Sister Anne's soft grip and lunge for the hallway behind Uncle Rayson, for I fear I don't have a chance to get past Father Gabriel himself.

But Uncle Rayson is faster than I thought. I knew he's strong. I knew he's cruel. But I had no idea he's quick. He reaches out and grabs me, his bony, hot fingers wrapping around my neck, freezing me in his grasp.

"You thought you could escape *me*, child? I, who have crushed the bodies and souls of men far greater and stronger than you?"

He laughs, a shrill, cruel sound. Uncle Rayson turns me around so I'm staring directly at Father Gabriel. Rayson tightens his grip, his long, sharp nails biting into my skin as he forces me to my knees.

I struggle against him, but every time I move, his nails sink deeper into my neck. My blood drips down and soaks into my collar.

Father Gabriel sighs. "If she's going to try to escape like Sister Kathryn did, she's not worth the trouble," says the tall man in white, his voice sad, his eyes filled with pity and regret. "She could have lived a happy life here, but maybe it's better this way. Maybe her death will be more profitable than her life. We'll make a spectacle of her body for all the youth to see. Let them know what happens if they try to flee. For she really is a homely thing, and her children would be, as well."

It hurts to hear him talk of me like that, even though I'd rather die than bear their children. To have them taken from my breast. Even so, the thought of death fills me with dread. It sets my mind racing, trying to think of a way to escape once again.

"You are a wise and benevolent father," Uncle Rayson says, bowing his head, keeping his grip firm. "Your word is law."

"Squeeze her neck until your fingers crush her bones and the ugly thing falls from her shoulders and rolls across the floor." A sick smile spreads across Father Gabriel's face, bloodlust shining in his rage-filled eyes.

"As you wish, my lord," Uncle Rayson says, wasting no time getting to his task.

I thrash about, trying to pry his hands from my neck, but it's no use. He's stronger than a man should be, and no matter how hard I try, I can't free myself.

Pain erupts in a horseshoe around my neck. Everywhere his fingers dig into my flesh, the pain like bruises building upon bruises. My heartbeat thu-thump thu-thump thu-thumps where the arteries are restricted. My muscles bulge as he closes his fists around my neck.

Pent-up blood splashes out and down my chest, splattering Father Gabriel's pristine white robe, leaving bright crimson dots that form constellations upon the silky cloth. He steps back so as not to wet his shoes in the puddle of red growing beneath me.

Uncle Rayson crushes my neck, making my head wobble. I can no longer keep it steady. I've lost all control. Despair floods my mind. My eyes no longer close. My hands dangle useless at my sides. I've lost all rights over my own body.

My vision grows dark and fuzzy. Thick spit fills my mouth and traces lines down my chin. A gurgling sound escapes my crushed throat. A stream of blood-tinged snot races from my nose and pours into my mouth, the salt and copper of it bitter on my swelling tongue. The last thing I see before my spine pops with a loud crack and my world is thrown into the dark is the look of pure disgust on Father Gabriel's face. My last act before I die is finding solace in the fact I turned that smile into a grimace.

*****

Try again. Turn to page 54.

I'm tired of waiting, and I must hurry before Sister Anne returns. I jump up to get out, but whatever has been poured into the water to make it smell so good has made the bottom of the tub slippery, and my foot slides out from under me.

I try to catch myself from falling, but I can't find any traction, and my body pitches backward. My arms pinwheel, trying to grab anything to stop my fall, but there's nothing there but air.

The back of my head slams hard on the tub's porcelain edge with a loud crack and I slump beneath the water.

Blood pours out from my skull, and it's drifting up and mixing into the water, a beautiful hue as my eyes blink beneath the swirling red lines.

My thoughts are all mixed up. Part of me knows I need to get up, the pressure building in my lungs, but I can't remember why, and I'm so dizzy it hurts to move my head. I don't think I even can rise because my arms are just floating things that feel too far away to be useful.

So I decide to stay. It's warm here and I feel safe. I decide to breath.

*****

The correct answer was to wait. Turn to page 20.

"Ma, I can't. I'm sorry. They'll hurt you and it'll be my fault," I tell her.

She opens her mouth to protest, but I don't give her time. I turn and head into the entryway, where Pa still stands, blocking the men outside from coming in.

"Ruby, please," Ma begs, but quietly, not wanting to be heard. Not wanting to make things worse for us. Worse for her and Pa and Little Joe or Sammie, wherever he's being held.

"It's okay, Pa. I'll go," I say, placing a hand on his large shoulder. Trying to reassure him as best I can, though I can feel how bad he's shaking.

"No, Ruby," Pa says, indecision burning in his eyes. Wanting to keep me here and keep me safe, but knowing if he does anything against these men, we'll all be punished. And the price will be a high one.

"There now, Joseph. You've raised a good one, here," Uncle Rayson says, his shrewd eyes ablaze. "An obedient one. You should be proud."

Uncle Rayson looks me up and down, cataloging me in a way he never has before. There's also disappointment etched in the lines of his aging wrinkled face. For Pa was right when he called me plain, a thing I had been secretly proud of until now. Thinking it would keep me from the Big House.

"Just tell me, please, what is it Father Gabriel wants with her? I must know, for I can't bear it if I don't," Pa says, his hand on my shoulder as I move before him, standing between him and our unwanted guests.

"It is not our place to question Father Gabriel or his wishes," Brother Paul says from behind Uncle Rayson in his soft voice. "For he is the all-knowing, and he leads us with great—"

"Give it a rest, Brother Paul," Uncle Rayson says, rolling his eyes and stepping forward, grabbing my wrist with sharp and bony fingers. "For Joseph here is not a stupid man." Uncle Rayson stares Pa straight in the eyes like he wishes Pa would do a thing he would need redeeming of. Something about that look says Uncle Rayson would love to be the one to help Pa find redemption. "Samuel, through his actions, caused us to lose a Chosen Daughter, and so your family must replace her. We must teach our youth the importance of obedience. We must warn them away from the evil tools of the outside world. There must be consequences for their actions, for otherwise, they will never learn."

Pa's eyes are full of tears and so much sorrow. "You won't chain her up or take her tongue, will you?"

"Nay, nay," Uncle Rayson says, his voice gentler now as he pulls me down the single stair from our porch onto the cement walkway. "For she has ever always been an obedient child and there is no need for it, is there?" He speaks this to me, his eyes looking deep into mine.

I drop my gaze to the ground. I have no strength to speak. I just nod and follow, not looking back as they lead me away. I can't bear the thought of seeing Pa standing there, looking like he did when they took Sammie down this same short walk. Pa has always been a strong man. A proud man. But that day Sammie was taken, he became a broken one. And I cannot bear to see him so again because of a choice I made.

***

I'm in the back seat of a shiny black car, wedged between Uncle Rayson and Brother Paul, baking in the heat coming off their bodies. Uncle Rayson burns with an intensity that makes me uncomfortable. It's almost like if I were to reach out with my finger, its tip would burn when it touched his skin. And with that heat, there's also a sense of electricity sparking off him. It scares me how almost otherworldly it is. How inhuman.

Brother Paul feels safer, so I scoot as much as I can to his side, even though there is no real space for me to do so. There is no way to not be touching either of them on this short ride from my family's small home to the Big House.

The Big House is where Father Gabriel and a few of the unmarried Elders like Uncle Rayson live. It's also where the Chosen Daughters live. These are the girls picked by Father Gabriel himself to continue the lineage of the Elders. For when the end of things comes, we'll need an army to survive the aftermath. We'll need an army to rebuild. Or so it has been ingrained in us since childhood. But now, I wonder.

If Katie could run and escape, can I? Is the end really coming or is there another life I could live out there in the great big world beyond the tiny community I've known? Could I have the same choices as the girls and women Sammie and Katie were always talking about from those videos on his phone? And could I ever find the same strength that Katie had? Be that kind of brave?

I'm nearly crying when the car pulls to a stop outside the Big House; I'm so afraid and filled with indecision. I'm so scared about what happens once I walk up those steps and through that door. What will become of me? What will they make me do?

Should I run when they let me leave this car? Should I turn and flee into the woods as Katie had? Praying all the while I can make it to a place I can be free. Free of this world and all these people. Free from the ever-threatening gaze of Uncle Rayson and from all the strict rules we must follow to stay on the path of the righteous.

Or should I for now accept my fate and see what's waiting for me beyond that dark threshold? If I enter, maybe I can find out how Sammie is, for we haven't had news of him for months. It would lighten my heart some to know he's okay. To know he's still alive. And if he's in a cell way down deep, maybe I can find a way to see him. To lighten his heart some, too.

Maybe I can find a way to set him free.

*****

Flee through the woods as Katie had. Turn to page 18.

Stay and see what happens. Turn to page 50.

The hall before me seems to grow longer as I step into it, its doors stretching on forever. The hallway makes the most sense. There was a stairwell going up connected to it, so there must be one going down.

The first door I encounter opens, but inside is a plain square room with boxes stored from floor to ceiling. The next room is the same, only instead of boxes, piles of stacked chairs fill one side, and disassembled beds lean against the opposite wall.

Behind the third door, I expect more useless junk. But it's filled with small cages, stacked three or four high. Inside them, things move around, but I can't tell what or how many. There's no way down inside this room, but I'm too curious. I step inside, my eyes glued to the closest cage, squinting to better see under the dim flickering light from the lanterns in the hall.

I take a small step inside. The cage is the size of what Ma used to keep baby chicks in after they hatched. About three feet by three, made of some sort of silvery mesh. Whatever's inside must need a lot of air, because I can't understand why else it'd be in a cage like this.

I wish I had a light with me. Something to give me a better look.

Then there's a flash of bright color, yellow or maybe orange, and something falls on the back of my neck. It feels like tiny sticks tapping on me. I slap whatever it is, and a sharp prick of pain lights a fire in my neck. Whatever landed on me wraps itself around my hand, and a thousand tiny legs scratch at my fingers. There's another jab in my palm, followed by another bright stabbing of heat up my arm.

Dizzy, I fall forward into the cage, smack off it and land on the floor. The cage lands on top of me. Out of a large gash in its mesh, a long centipede slithers out, its many legs working, looking like a wave of yellow and red and orange as it runs across my chest, biting me through my thin gown.

The bites burn so bad that I start to scream. As soon as my mouth opens, another centipede scrambles over my chin, its pointy legs forcing their way past my lips.

I grab hold of it with my unwounded hand. My other is swollen and blazes with fire. The centipede nearly wiggles all the way into my mouth, but I don't let go even as pincers dig into the soft flesh of my inner arm and another centipede forces its way into my nose. The one in my mouth bites, slips through my fingers, and obstructs my breathing as it works its way down my throat.

Its feet scratch their way deeper and deeper, my throat swelling around it. My nose is closed by the other. And over my entire body, more of them rush around, pricking me wherever they can. How many were inside that little cage? No wonder they're so angry.

My face hurts, it's grown so tight, and the bitter venom from the centipede filling my throat flows into my lungs as if someone poured acid inside me. Everywhere I feel agony. Nothing moves without exploding in the most awful feeling.

It takes too long for my vision to fade. Time slows as I writhe, drool and urine leaking from me, tears streaming from my puffed-up eyes. It takes too long for my body to give up the fight and for my heart to finally stop beating. Too long for me to finally die.

*****

Try again. Turn to page 25.

The first demon comes closer, and I act without thinking. "To the water, c'mon!"

"Alright, let's go! Hurry!" Sammie cries, but I can barely hear him over the din of the water and the demon's wings beating the air.

I pull Sammie toward the water's edge. We pause just long enough to look each other in the eyes before I grab his hand and jump.

We plunge into water that is cold and fast. Sammie's hand is torn away as the current takes him from me. I don't know which way is up, and I spin in the churning water. My body bashes against stone as I'm pulled downstream and my chest cries out for air.

I try to calm myself and let my body float to the surface. Just as my face breaks free for me to suck in air, my head hits a stalagmite. I hit it so hard, that part of my jaw caves in and pain explodes inside my head. I taste blood and I suck in a lungful of water and broken teeth as I'm plunged under once more. Everything swirls around me, the world in motion, and I can't stop myself from moving with it.

My leg hits something hard and the bone cracks, erupting in so much agony I open my mouth to scream, flooding my throat with water. My lungs burn, which makes no sense because it's water filling them up and not fire. Then my arm cracks against a pile of stones.

I try coughing, but underneath the surface, all I do is pull more water in. Everything grows darker, but before I drift away, my head collides with something hard. This time it's not my jaw that caves in, but the base of my skull. And with it, the final darkness comes and my pain is gone.

*****

The correct answer was to turn left and head for the cave.
Turn to page 7.

I keep running down the stairs. I won't give up! Not when I must be so close to the bottom. So close to Sammie.

"Leave me alone!" I yell.

There's a burst of coldness all around me, then the air grows warmer, but just as thick with a sour smell as was before. The spirit has gone.

A few more steps and I hit slippery cold stone, sending me tumbling onto the floor. I've made it to the bottom, my dress ripped at the knees, which feel a small kiss of pain where I've skinned them.

I look back up, expecting to see nothing but steps going up and up and up, but instead there's candlelight flickering through the outline of the door leading into the kitchen. I've gone the distance of a single story in what felt like an eternity. I'm so grateful for Auntie Ruth. For her wisdom and her kindness.

In this room, candles are lit along the wall, burning in shiny brass holders, dripping wax that disappears before it reaches the floor. This is a magical place, and it terrifies me.

There's the sound of moving water somewhere ahead, probably the source of the smell. But the scent of death is so overwhelming I gag and wonder if that's part of the magic, too. Part of the attempt to keep those who aren't welcome here away. If it's not, and that smell's coming from dead bodies, then it makes me even more worried for Sammie. The thought that he could be one of the dead things making that horrid smell snaps me back into reality.

To my left, the way Auntie Ruth told me would lead to him, there's a door a little farther down. It's heavy and made of thick wood slabs held together with tarnished metal bands and crude bolts. It's a door made to keep people out. Or in. The door to a dungeon.

It has a handle made of twisted iron that doesn't want to budge, so I dig into the rough cobblestone with my bare feet and push as hard as I can. It takes all my effort for it to slowly swing inward, scraping against the uneven floor.

The room inside is lined with tiny cells sealed by doors similar to the size and strength as the one I just opened. Each one has a large opening with thick black bars, and a keyhole in a tarnished plate below a twisted metal handle. There must be close to twenty cells in this place, and I can't remember which one she said Sammie is in.

There's no sign of a guard, or that anyone can hear me, but I keep my voice down, calling out Sammie's name, hoping with every inch of my tattered being that he's okay. That he's in here, waiting for me to rescue him. "Samuel, please! Answer me if you're here. Please, Sammie. Please be okay."

Tears stream down my face as I listen for him.

Someone whimpers in a cell to my left. "The mother's coming for me. The father, too," a woman says. "I've sinned too much to be redeemed. Uncle Rayson says so. Uncle Rayson's tried."

She says this over and over again, getting louder with each word, then suddenly quieter again, barely audible over the constant sound of running water.

"She's coming for me. He is, too. They're gonna eat my soul. Gobble it up. Uncle Rayson made it as clean as he could. He used my pain to bleach out the darkness within, but he couldn't get all the spots out. Couldn't get it good enough. I'm unclean. My soul is unclean. They'll eat it up and I'll be empty. Empty! Empty!"

She goes on and on and on, each word a dagger in my mind. Poking me. Spearing me.

Part of me finds her voice familiar. I've heard it at some church meeting, maybe. But it's not one I know well enough to conjure a face.

I search for the keys to these tiny cells and pray to the gods I'm not sure I believe in for her to stop talking. Or at least stick to the soft crazed whispers, instead of the ear-splitting screams.

There, just to the right of the door I came through is a simple hook, and on it, a large silver ring with a single ornate key. I don't see any other hooks or keys dangling anywhere along this wall, and all the other walls are lined with cells. This one must open them all. I'm grateful, because the idea of having to go through a bunch of keys as fast as I can to find the one that would open whatever door my brother's behind makes sweat pop up on my neck.

The woman continues her irritating babble, and I feel as if my mind will explode from the pressure growing in it.

"Sammie! Are you here?" I call.

Everything quiets except the water rushing away nearby. The woman has stopped.

The smell is even worse than it was out in the hall. The stench of urine burns my nose and makes my eyes tear, and there's that other smell, too. The one you make when you're sick, when everything you eat comes out and the heat from it burns as it pours outta you.

I grab the key, remembering Auntie Ruth's instructions, and rush across the room, hoping it's the cell Auntie Ruth was talking about because that nasty smell is going to make Ma's meatloaf rise up inside me. Dinner wants out and I'm not sure how much longer I can hold it in. My head pounds from the way the prisoner's voice beats against it and I just want to be outta this place as soon as I can.

"Sammie!" I try again, banging on the door.

There's a rustle in the cell to my right as the woman's bony fingers slide through the opening in the door. They wrap around the bars, the flesh translucent, with bright blue lines of veins tracing their way up and over swollen knuckles.

"Sammie!" the woman's voice shrieks, the sound like daggers to my ears. "Sammie! Sammie! Sammie!" Her crooked nose and sharp chin poke out as her mouth presses against those bars, baring blackened, broken shards of teeth.

"Ruby?" another voice says before getting swallowed up by the woman's yells.

Happy tears flow from my eyes. My heart is filled with relief. It's him. It's finally him. My brother, after all these weeks of not knowing. Of fearing he was dead. My hands shake so bad I almost drop the key trying to fit it in the lock. "I'm here, Sammie. I'm here. Are you okay?"

"Ruby? It's really you! But, how? Why? I don't understand." My brother is at the door, his hands wrapping around the bars.

The shrieking has stopped, but I can hear the woman breathing. Panting away.

The key turns in the lock with a sharp click. The woman whispers now, so low I can't tell what she's saying. I only hear the rise and fall of her words, so soft and tragically beautiful. It's a desperate sound. A sad sound.

Sammie pushes the door open and rushes out, wrapping me up in his arms and twirling me around. The rough fabric of his woolen brown robe scratches my skin through the thin gown.

I squeeze him tight. "You're okay! Ma and Pa and I have been so scared. I'm so glad you're okay!"

"I am! I'm fine!" he says, but he's wobbly on his feet. "I could use a heaping plate of Ma's spaghetti, is all. And a nice tall glass of ice water would sure hit the spot."

He laughs, so I laugh too. The sound of it mixes together and reminds me of all those times as kids. He and I and Katie, laughing about the stuffy way the Elders looked in their fancy white robes, or how Uncle Rayson looked all uppity all the time. Those innocent days back before Katie was chosen and ripped from our carefree lives. A sadness seeps into my heart. The same memories must creep into Sammie's mind as well, because his laugh grows heavy, and then stops. Same as mine.

"We need to find the way out of here," I tell him.

"Out? You're going out?" the woman says. "Take me! Let me be free! I'll show you the way, for you'll never find it on your own." She reaches a thin arm through the bars, her fingers stretching toward us, the nails ragged and bitten down, covered in dried blood and grime. "Please don't leave me here. Don't leave poor Auntie Martha here all alone."

"Auntie Martha?" I say, the name taking me back to one of the scariest times of our lives. Back when kids went missing one by one and nobody knew why or how it was happening?

Sammie limps to the door, the only exit from the room, as the memory returns and disgust creeps across my spine. For Auntie Martha baked kids into pies and dropped their bones in the broth pot and fed the rest of them to the hogs. She was in charge of the kitchens back then. Nobody knows how many of us were fed her stolen children at the community gatherings. Most of which were held to show our support for the families of the missing littles.

She would steal them away as they played near the woods, their parents' backs turned for the briefest of time. Or she would take them as they walked the trails to classes or back home. Always waiting patiently for one to straggle behind the others, smiling when whoever was in charge would say, "Thomas was just there!" or "Eliza couldn't have been out of my sight for more than a second!" Always they were taken without crying out or making any noise at all.

For a while, there were whispers that a wild demon had crawled its way out of the pits beneath us to feed on the naughty. A rumor the Elders wanted us to believe. I heard Ma and Pa talking about it back in hushed tones, pressing my ear against their bedroom door, my curiosity beating out the fear of getting caught.

They didn't know who was taking the kids, but they hated the idea of us being afraid of demons, something I don't think they really believed in. I learned a lot that night, a lot about their distrust of Father Gabriel, and especially of Uncle Rayson. For they believed it was Rayson who was taking them and Father Gabriel allowed it. They believed it was for some secret ritual, or just because Uncle Rayson was a man of pure evil who enjoyed the darkness that came with inflicting pain.

After hearing them talk, I didn't know what to believe. Nights were spent lying in bed afraid of the rabid demon running through our land, snatching up those who had gone against our teaching. Ripping us apart with their razor-sharp claws and drinking our blood to satisfy their thirst. But in the day, when the sun was bright and the demons of the darkness seemed impossible, I believed it was Uncle Rayson stealing us to do terrible things. Painful things. Scary things.

None of us were prepared for the truth. None of us who knew Auntie Martha could ever have predicted what she was doing. We ate her soups with silver spoons and marveled at the taste. We took huge servings of her meat pies and thick stews and gravy-covered roasts and none of us ever suspected a thing.

It wasn't until one of the Sisters who minded the fires walked in on her holding the severed head of little Sarah Winters by its thick, curly hair, ripping at the swollen tongue with a pair of crude tongs.

"Mad Martha?" I turn toward the woman's cell. Begging to be let go. Promising to lead us out of here. But helping her escape is a scary thought.

"Please girl, please! Let me out, let me go!" Her voice is shrill, drilling into my head, each syllable a sharp point against my brain. "I'll show you the way and keep you from triggering the traps! I've heard them talking. Always talking, as if I'm not here. I know what's out there. What's down them tunnels. I know what is real and what's just for show."

"We need to go. Just leave her here," Sammie says, pulling my hand. "She's crazier now than she ever was. All she does is rant and scream. All day and night. I can't wait to get away from her. I haven't slept more than an hour at a time since being thrown in that... that... that cell. It's been so hard, Ruby. I have to get away from her." His eyes beg me to go with him, to leave her behind.

"What if she can help?" I ask. "What if she really *can* get us out of here? If she knows the way?"

"Yes! The way! I know the way!" Her hands are back on the bars, her eyes bright and crazed. "Please! I can't stand it in here.

They made me do it, you know? Sacrifice those babes. They needed us to feed on the flesh of the innocent for some spell to work. Some ceremony none of us were to know about. It was a sacrifice to our gods we're not let in on. Our gods demand our souls, and if we knew that, if the parents of the young knew the blood of their babies would be required, none of them would stay. Well, most of them wouldn't, anyway. It wasn't my fault. I did what I was told and then my payment for it was this cell. This dungeon. This shitty smelling room where I was meant to rot day after week after month after year. I can't take it anymore. I can't. Please, let me free. Let me go."

By the end of all this she's begging, no longer screaming at us, but pleading. To slide the key into her door and let her into the world.

I'm afraid of making our way out alone. Auntie Ruth made it sound dangerous. The thing on the stairs was probably just a small taste of that danger. If Mad Martha is our way to freedom, I should trust her. Part of me believes what she says, about being forced into it. About being made to murder those children and present them to us in great porcelain serving dishes.

"She's mad, Ruby. She's crazy," Sammie says. "You can't trust her to show us out this door, let alone the way out from the basement. Let's just go while we can. Before they come to check and catch us here."

Sammie's voice is just as desperate as Martha's, but he wasn't on the stairs. He didn't hear the voice warning me about things that could rip me apart.

So what do I do? Do I let her free? Or do I listen to Sammie and leave this place without her?

*****

Unlock her door and hope she leads us out of here, safe and sound, as she says she will. Turn to page 44.

Turn to page 44.

Leave her be as Sammie says we must. We'll find our way out on our own. Turn to page 83.

It may not be Martha's fault she did what she did. These evil men manipulate us all, not giving us any real free will. We obey, or we die.

"We need her help," I tell Sammie.

"Don't do it, Ruby."

I go to her cell and push the key into the lock. There's a loud click as it unlocks, and Martha pushes the door open. I barely jump out of the way in time, but Sammie's not so lucky, falling to the floor.

No sooner than she's out of her cell, she's on me. Her long, thin fingers are hooks that dig into my eyes, sliding over and down around them, pulling them out of my head with two squelching, popping sounds, one right after the other.

My face erupts in agony. "My eyes!"

I bring my hands up, but Mad Martha's fingers close into fists around my eyeballs, and she pulls them free with two quick yanks. My head is tugged forward, and I almost fall.

Sammie shouts at her to stop, but she slurps and chews my eyeballs. "Fresh meat, fresh meat! After all this time, fresh meat!" she cries, her voice filled with glee. "Oh, how I missed the taste of it."

I fall to my knees as Sammie struggles with Martha, yelling and screaming he's going to kill her.

One of them trips over my feet and thuds onto the floor beside me. I pray it was Martha, but that's her chuckling above me.

"Stupid boy," she says, before her fingers twist into my hair and thrust my head back.

Mad Martha's broken teeth sink into my neck. The flesh rips as she jerks her head away.

I land in a heap on the floor, my hand feeling at the hole Mad Martha left behind with her blackened broken teeth. A jagged hole where blood spills free, spraying with each beat of my heart.

My heart rate slows and my blood empties onto the stone floor. My mind fades into the nothingness around us. Into the void that exists between this world and the next. Into the forever darkness.

*****

The correct answer was to leave her be. Turn to page 83.

I rip my hand free from Sister Anne's and run straight at Father Gabriel, hoping to catch him off guard and zip around him.

This man who claims to be a lesser god raises his hand and closes it into a fist.

Even though I'm still a few feet away from him, I'm instantly stopped, my arms stuck at my sides, palms flattened against thighs, toes pointing straight down toward the floor I'm floating inches above.

I want to scream, to curse at him, at both of them. A lifetime of anger builds up inside me. Anger at being told what to do and see and feel and think every second of every day. And all because of fear. Fear of noncompliance. Fear of these two men. But I can't. I can't let out all that pent-up frustration because my mouth is sealed shut. It's as stuck as the rest of me, and I'm as helpless before Father Gabriel as I've always been. As we all have been.

"I'm so tired of the young," he says with a roll of his eyes. He walks around me, taking me in, his shoes clicking against the hardwood. Stopping only when he's back where he started. "Every few generations it starts, and we have to deal with it once again. Over and over back through time and it's exhausting." Sorrow drips from his voice.

"They forget, my lord. They forget that the end will come someday, and we need to stay together. We need to stay strong and continue to build toward that future. To the coming of our fallen angels. To the end of things as we know them," Uncle Rayson says.

My eyes are frozen in place, same as the rest of my body, but I can still see all the same, and wishing I couldn't. I hate the sight of them staring at me, considering what to do. A single tear slips from my right eye. My left burns and begs to be blinked, but there's nothing I can do. Nothing but wait.

"We'll have to remind them. We'll have to show them what's at stake." Father Gabriel turns. The front door opens without a hand being placed on it. He walks through it, and I float along after.

Down the steps we go. Once he's at the bottom, he stops and gestures before him. My body obeys his command, floating up into the air high above the road, turning as I pass him, so I see his face, or that he may see mine, my arms forced straight up and out so I resemble the cross of the Jesus worshipers. Father Gabriel makes a circle motion with his hand, and I flip upside down with a jerk, my hair fanning out below me. Another tear falls from my eye, running down my forehead and dropping onto the road.

The blood rushes to my head, which begins to throb. I don't know how long it is before Father Gabriel loses interest and walks away. I don't know how long it is before I lose consciousness.

I wake later in the same position, my head hurting, my throat and eyes dry, my tongue a useless, painful thing within my mouth. The day drones on and I remain motionless, unable to sleep because my eyes are always open. The sun beats down on me and the sweat mixes in with the hot smelly urine that flows down my torso and around my chin. I itch everywhere, and I cannot scratch. My head throbs and my kidneys ache and my eyes burn but there's nothing I can do about any of it.

None of that is the worst part of this slow demise. None of it compares to the feeling in my heart as it breaks at the sight of Ma and Pa and Little Joe. The entire community has been gathered below me. I heard my mother's screams before I saw her, and my new tears bring relief to my dry eyes.

"My poor Ruby, no!" Pa shouts.

Little Joe is crying as Ma screams over and over. No words, just grief let out in long mournful wails.

"My family," Father Gabriel says, his voice rising above the crowd noise.

Everyone quiets except Pa, who begs Ma to hush for Joe's sake.

"My children," Father Gabriel says, once he has complete silence. "I've gathered you here this morning to pray. Pray for the soul of this young girl who betrayed us all. For she was going to leave us. Abandon us as we prepare for the coming of our fallen angels. As we do the hard work of preparing for the after times. For the end of things."

The crowd boos. I feel the stinging pain of rocks thrown at me, except for where my feet and legs have grown too numb to feel. Pa consoles Ma as best he can, all the while Little Joe cries.

"Now, now," Father Gabriel goes on. "It is not our place to judge this misguided child, for she knows not how great is her sin. It's our job to learn from her mistakes, and guide our young away from this most horrendous path. For every brother or sister we lose is a threat to our new beginning and we must not forget our place in the new world that's yet to come. For every brother or sister who leaves us, leaves to find their deaths in what's to be, and when they come crawling back for help at the dawn of the new civilization, they will be denied entrance. The eternal garden is only for the true believers. It's only for the ones whose souls have been washed clean in the water of our holy spring."

The crowd erupts into wild cheers that spike the pain in my head.

"So let this poor girl's remaining hours be a cruel reminder to the young. We are your family, and you are ours, and without us you will wither away and be left out in the elements. You will die, as she will die, without us. And you will lament as her family does." With these last words, Father Gabriel turns to Ma and Pa and Little Joe, huddled together, holding each other. He shakes his head as if they are the greatest of disappointments, then turns and walks up the steps into the Big House, leaving everyone talking and whispering and staring at me until, eventually, they also leave.

Over the days, my mother stays as long as she can. She sings to me the songs she used to sing, back when I was just a girl. She tells me the stories I always loved, but mostly, she cries. My father doesn't come at all, just Ma. And I know it's because he can't bear it. He can't bear seeing me like this, fading away, as Ma must. Watching my body dry up and burn in the sun. That's the worst part about this. The part that breaks my heart. Watching her pain as she watches me die.

The last thing I see before I fade away from this life, as the pain throbs on and on and on in all the parts of me that remain capable of feeling anything, is her face. Swollen from crying. Her hair disheveled from days of pulling at it. Her plain clothes dirty, stained from kneeling and sleeping on the ground when she could no longer stand. When she was too tired to make it home for the night.

The last thing I see before the darkness seeps in, is her praying to whatever gods she still believes in. I wonder if they're the same gods she told me of.

I wonder if I'll see them soon. I wonder if I'll see anything at all.

*****

Try again. Turn to page 54.

Both choices are terrifying, but to think I'm finally so close to Sammie is too great a thing to turn away from. I need to know he's safe. I need to know he's okay. And I know he's in there, somewhere.

Running away comes as an almost overwhelming urge, but I must stay on course, at least for now, and make them think I'm going along with it all. There will be time to flee later. After I know about Sammie. After I know he's okay. And hopefully, I can take him with me.

Uncle Rayson's door is opened for him, and he scoots out with the agility of a snake. He doesn't pause before walking up the stairs to where a white-robed Father Gabriel awaits on the stoop before the open door. I know I'm supposed to be sliding out, and I want to, but my body is frozen for a second, my heart racing, my hands shaking.

"Hurry, girl. For you don't want to keep Father Gabriel waiting," Brother Paul says as he gently nudges me toward the open door. "He has infinite love for us, but not infinite patience."

Part of me is grateful for the kindness I sense in this man. The Elders are not always known for their good will, so feeling his genuine care gives me the strength to scoot across the empty seat and step out.

I have walked by this great house countless times. The gathering hall is a little farther down through the woods and the path from my family's home goes right in front of the Big House. I've often stood in the shadows of the trees on my way to help in the kitchens on celebration days and wondered what it was like to live within these walls. So close to *him*. So close to our leader, Father Gabriel.

The house seems so much bigger now, as I stand at the bottom of the stairs, looking up at where Uncle Rayson turns, standing one step below Father Gabriel. Both looking down at me. I can feel the steely ice from Father Gabriel's gaze the same as the fiery heat coming from Uncle Rayson's beady black eyes. I feel both cold and hot as I begin the long walk up the steps. The closer to them I get, the smaller I feel, shrinking inside myself as they loom above me. It takes all my will to continue on, to not just turn and go. The fear is building with each slow step and my heart is like a rabbit in my chest, thumping, running, trying to break free.

"Welcome, Chosen One. I hope you find your time here to be fruitful and pleasant," Father Gabriel says, his voice like silk. He steps back and motions with a wide swing of his arm for me to enter. The doorway leads into pitch-black darkness, not a single candle or lamp lit.

"Thank you," I say, so low I'm not sure it makes it to his ears. I enter the house, the cold chilling me straight through. Not even Uncle Rayson's burning gaze can reach me in here. I'm filled with nothing but ice and dread as I make my way farther into the darkness, the house eating me all up.

I finally stop, not wanting to walk into anything I can't see, not knowing which way to go or where to turn. Behind me, Father Gabriel's shoes make hollow tapping sounds as he walks across the hardwood. He puts a heavy hand on my shoulder. It's so cold it could be a dead man's. The coolness of it sinks into my arm like it's turning me into ice. I want to knock it off me and run back out the door and keep on running until my feet can't go no more.

I turn toward the rectangle of light that leads outside just as Uncle Rayson swings the door closed behind him. The only way out I know is shut with a loud thump and a click as he slides a key into the lock and twists. Maybe they've always locked the door from both sides, but I'm guessing it was added after Katie's escape.

We stand here, none of us talking, and I can feel the darkness pressing in on me. As if it's sizing me up. As if it's not just the absence of light but the presence of something *more*. And all the while Father Gabriel's hand is still there, heavy on my shoulder, a shoulder numb from the bitter cold seeping into me.

We stand in silence, each second feeling like an hour.

"Sister Anne," Father Gabriel calls. "The lamps have gone out. Can you relight them?"

"Yes, Father," a woman says somewhere to my left, her voice so docile, so subservient.

I hadn't known we weren't alone and I jump, though barely, as I'm still weighed down by Father Gabriel's otherworldly hand. A match is struck and a tiny reddish-orange glow blooms to life in the small hands of a woman not much older than I. She's beautiful, even in the small amount of light she holds, her hand cupped to keep the tiny flicker alive as she approaches a domed lantern hanging high on the wall. She twists a tiny knob and pokes the match through a small hole in the metal beneath the glass.

The entire room is revealed to me. There's a long hall through an archway just ahead, and to my right and left larger rooms branch off, lost in their own thick shadows. The flickering lamplight stops short of those two rooms as if by magic, or fear of entering. If light can feel fear, that is.

Looking into those shadows is like looking into the worst possibilities all rolled into one. As if the house is whispering to me, telling me not to enter. Not to step my foot into them without first being told I can. I finally understand why more folk don't try to run and flee. To take their children into the night and rush them away to other parts of the world beyond where our Family lives.

Because Father Gabriel is *real*. Everything he's taught us is *real*. It's why more don't try and escape this place. Why we suffer Uncle Rayson and his cruel redemption. Why we follow all the rules set down before us.

Because these aren't just men who stand next to me, oh no. They really are the spawn of the ancient evil ones. They are of the bloodline passed down, generation after generation, to one day walk the earth after the end has come and gone. To reclaim what's left and to usher in the rebirth of the fallen angels that we bow our heads to every Sunday.

All these thoughts flow through my mind and I can sense the house itself whispering to me. Telling me it's true. It's all true.

I sense it laughing as my will to flee weakens. Fear rushes through the chilled blood in my veins. It makes me want to fall onto my knees and pray to them. To the fallen angels.

I want to kiss Father Gabriel's shoes and beg him to take mercy on me and my damaged soul. To wash away all my sins and thank him for the gift he's given in bringing me here. In choosing *me*, even though my looks betray me.

And though the entryway is lit, the darkness from those other rooms reaches out to me, presses against me. It's this darkness whispering to me, not the house itself. I can feel it. And just as my knees wobble and I'm about to fall, my mind on the verge of breaking, of crumbling into a million worthless pieces, Father Gabriel removes his hand.

The chill seeping through me vanishes as if it was never there at all. The shadows through the doorways turn to plain shadows. There are no voices, no whispers of ungodly truths. I am just a girl, standing here next to a man. A man who seems not to age, but not some usher of the end.

My legs still shake, and though I feel more myself again, the terror is worse than it has been since they took my brother. And part of me knows I need to run, that things here are not okay. If Katie could make it out, so can I.

"Take our newest Chosen Daughter to be bathed and wash away the dirt of the outside, for she is one of you now," Father Gabriel says to Sister Anne. "Then feed her if she's hungry and place her in Sister Katie's old room. She will be baptized soon, and will fill the need that's been left wanting."

Sister Anne nods before reaching out and sliding her soft, warm hand around my own and gently pulling me toward the hall.

But I don't want to go. I don't want to follow her to whatever future these men have lined up for me. I don't want to be bound to a bed to do their bidding. To give them child after child until

I'm all used up, then tossed away to serve the wives of the married Elders who live outside these walls. Sister Anne pulls me toward a destiny my mind rises up against.

Do I follow her now, or rip free from her and make a break for it through one of these other shadowy rooms? The way behind me is locked tight, the key in Uncle Rayson's robes.

Maybe I can find a back door or a window. I can find a way to do what Katie did. Either that, or I accept my fate and let Sister Anne lead me forward in hopes that I am safe this night, at least. Safe from *them*. Safe from the darkness that stole over me with Father Gabriel's icy touch. What choice should I make?

*****

Follow Sister Anne. It's crazy to think I can escape with both Father Gabriel *and* Uncle Rayson so close. Turn to page 60.

Head through the doorway to my left, past where Uncle Rayson stands. He's the smaller of the two and I can probably outrun him. Turn to page 26.

Run past Father Gabriel, through the doorway to my right. He'll never expect it, and I'll catch him off guard. There must be another way out. Turn to page 46.

The thought of fighting our way through these monsters is awful, but I'm afraid of what will happen if we try to force our way through the invisible wall.

"I can't go through there. I'm so sorry," I say, turning to Sammie, tears streaming down my face. "I'm too afraid we'll burn and die in the worst way ever."

"Okay, okay, we're okay," Sammie says, trying to comfort me as the mob of corpses closes in. "We can do it. I know we can."

"If we don't make it out of this, Sammie, I just want you to know you've been the most amazing brother a sister could ever ask for." I say these words as the papery skin-people flutter within reach.

"The feeling's mutual," he says. I hear the smirk in his voice again.

"That's our Sammie, always taking on life's challenges with a smile."

The husk of a corpse swings an empty fist at me, but I manage to snatch it and pull it toward me. It's unlike anything I've ever felt, soft and rough all at once, all dried out, but like it's been rubbed down with lotion, perhaps to keep it limber. To keep it from tearing itself to pieces when it moved.

It slaps me across the face with its free hand. It doesn't even hurt. It's just annoying. The fact that it has no bones or muscle makes it almost tickle.

I grab at the hand that's hitting me when a handful of the doll babies leap on Sammie. He screams and stumbles back. The thing in my grip brings its head up and into mine. The holes where its eyes once sat line up with my eyes. Before I know what's happening, it presses itself into me and over me, turning itself inside out over my body as if it's a glove.

Sammie's back is against the invisible barrier. The babies tear at him, their tiny hands climbing up the thick robe. He tries ripping free from whatever magic powers the invisible barricade while he swipes at the babies, but they keep coming. For every one he brushes away, two more replace it.

I want to run to him, to tear the babies off him, but the empty skin has rolled itself over my head and shoulders. It rips free from my grip and presses over me. This must be what it feels like to be eaten by a snake, only it's so dry in here, the skin absorbing my moisture as it covers me.

"Ruby, help! Pull me out!" Sammie screams, but it's all I can do to keep from falling as the husk inches down my body. "Get them off me!"

I want to call out to him, but the husk presses so close to my mouth that only muffled sounds escape. I get whatever air I can through the holes where its nostrils used to be. The hulking form of the elderly woman makes it to us, but now that I'm covered by the husk, she doesn't seem to see me as a threat.

She lunges at my brother, who's almost completely covered by babies. They bite into him, tearing away tiny chunks of his face and neck and arms and legs. They pull at his hair and claw at his flesh, and then the old woman presses herself into my brother, pushing him further into the invisible wall.

All the babies fall to the ground on this side of the barrier, and Sammie falls to the floor of the cave on the other. The monsters aren't able to penetrate it. They scramble against it. Try to get through. The woman beats her fists against the solid air keeping her from my brother.

I breathe so hard through those two tiny holes, trying to fight the skin that's covering me. I want to rip it off, but I can't move my arms or legs now that the husk has filled itself with my body. I want to bite at it from the inside, but it presses so perfectly against me I can't even move my lips, let alone my jaw.

All around me the monsters pass to press themselves against the end of the hall, trying to get at my brother. He stands on the other side of the invisible wall. Blood streams down his face and arms from all the bite marks, but otherwise he is okay.

Suddenly it feels as if a thousand needles are pricking into me. Whatever it is that's poking me works its way inside. It feels like tiny, long worms are forcing their way up my arms and legs and down my neck, shoulders and torso. Some crawl into my brain as others surround my heart. They inch their way inside me as if the husk is anchoring itself to me. To my heart and my mind. I'm afraid I know what's about to happen.

My thoughts change from wanting to free myself to figuring out a way to sever my tie to my own mind. I know it's not me thinking that.

My arm lifts and my fingers wiggle before my eyes, but it's not me who wiggles them. It's not me lifting my legs into the air, one after the other, as if to test them. And it's not me thinking the thoughts racing through my brain.

"Finally, after all this time," I say out loud, or at least, my body says. "It feels so good to be filled up." A sinister laugh is forced from my open mouth, and I feel dirty.

The worm-like things pump my blood outwards. They're arteries and veins, moving blood from my heart and into the flesh that holds me. It's becoming softer and something is secreted from it, covering my skin and dress. It touches everything but my lips and eyes, and everywhere I'm burning. It's like an acid eating away at me, leaving nerves and muscle and globs of fat unprotected. I am more exposed than I've ever been, powerless to protect myself.

A tear streams from a single eye, tracing its way down the outside of skin that's not mine. It's the last thing my body does for me. The last time I'm able to bend my will over what's always been mine. The tear trickles down the skin and falls from the face that's someone else's.

All over me now roots burrow in. They seal the skin with my body. They're taking over every part of me and making it their own.

In my mind, I'm shut behind a thousand impenetrable doors. I can't hear the thoughts anymore, from the new thing that's stolen me. It's as if I'm stuck inside a tiny little part of myself, unable to move or speak or even take a breath. I'm a consciousness only, doomed to watch my stolen body forever from eyes I no longer control. It's worse than death. It's hell.

*****

The correct answer was to turn back and find a way through the crowd of reanimated dead. Turn to page 93.

I stumble back, not wanting to take my eyes off the opening door. I trip over my own two feet, my legs all tangled up. My hands pinwheel, searching for something to grab to stop my fall. My left hand hits something on the counter, but I can't wrap my fingers around it. I'm falling too fast and all I do is pull it part way off the edge.

My butt, then my shoulders, smack the floor, but I'm able to keep my head from hitting too hard. I'm going to have some aches and pains from the bruises.

The door opens and someone steps through it, but at least I'm out of view. That's when I notice the heavy thing perched above me. It's sitting only about halfway on the counter and sways.

The person steps into the kitchen and suddenly I'm nervous about what will happen when they shut the door. I'm nervous the vibration will be just enough to send the thing crashing down on top of me. I start to roll away, but even before the door shuts, the large thing tips. A wooden butcher's block filled with knives.

A smaller knife slides out and turns end over end, its point plunging into my chest, followed by the full weight of the wooden cube behind it. The knife buries itself between my ribs, piercing my heart.

I gasp as the block topples onto my stomach and clunks onto the floor. My heart beats once more. I feel it jerk and stutter and be still. And then I feel nothing at all. Not even the cold of the darkness as it wraps itself around me.

*****

Try again. Turn to page 74.

I gently squeeze Sister Anne's soft hand and allow her to lead me down the darkened hall. It's an honest relief to be taken from those two men. From their coldness and the fire. Every step down the hall calms my mind a bit more. My heart beats a little less loud inside my chest. My nerves return. It would be madness to have tried running with them so close. I wouldn't have stood a chance.

"It will be nice to have someone new to talk to," Sister Anne whispers. "We weren't allowed to talk to Katie. They were afraid her ideas would spread among us. That she would poison us with her words of the outside world, so they took her tongue and locked her away."

I don't know what to say, but I don't want to start off by offending her, either. I recognize Sister Anne from our childhood, but the Chosen Daughters are picked years before they are taken, and once they are, they begin their training. They attend special classes outside of those the rest of us take. Their families are lifted in ranks, as well, and no longer socialize with those below them, as once they had. Part of me is honored to think someone as beautiful as her wants to be my friend, but another part is scared. Her kind has always shunned us lower ranks. Is she really that lonely here, that she would want to talk to me now?

I think about all the times we're allowed to see the Chosen Daughters once they leave their homes at the age of seventeen to come and live here, inside these walls I find myself trapped in now. At community dinners, sermons, and baptisms, they're made to stand off on their own, watching from a distance in their flowing sheer robes, so much more delicate than the thick off-white cotton ones we wear. They never sit, never talk, their heads cast down as if it is a sin to take in us common folk. Their faces are covered with a wispy veil that hides their features from us.

It makes me sad to think how lonely that must be. It makes me want to talk to her, offer her kinship, if only I could find the words. If only my mind wasn't filled with so many racing thoughts and fear of what is to come.

"Thank you," I manage because I don't know what else there is to say. I feel foolish for it. The Chosen Daughters are taught to speak with eloquence while the rest of us are instructed on how to can food and clean wounds and prepare for the new beginning. She must already think me a simpleton, and my face flushes when she stops in front of a large, closed door.

"Come, let's get you bathed and into something more comfortable," she says with a smile, twisting the knob and pushing open the door.

My eyes are shocked by a bathroom lit brightly by many burning lamps. Sister Anne must've prepared for my coming. The bath itself is filled with steaming water, accompanied by a strong scent of jasmine. There is no mirror above the sink, and I wonder why that is as she guides me in and tugs at the buttons running down the back of my dress.

"Do you know where my brother is? Samuel?" I ask, hoping Sister Anne remembers us from when we were little. Back when we were learning our letters and numbers and singing The Family's gospels in class.

"Hush," Sister Anne commands, her voice stern, but not unkind. "The first thing you need to learn here is that everything you say can be heard, no matter where you say it, or to who."

"I'm sorry," I tell her, looking into her eyes so she can see how scared I am for my brother. For me. "I just need to know if he's alive…"

Sister Anne's lips purse. I'm not sure what she's going to say, the way she glares at me. But then, just as I'm about to give up hope she'll take pity on me, she softens and walks to the door, poking her head into the hall as if checking to be sure we're alone. She closes the door.

"I really shouldn't say, I'm not sure they'd like it if I did, but I can't see the harm in it. Not really." She sighs and turns me back around while her fingers continue undoing my buttons.

"Samuel is fine. They keep him in the basement, in a cell. Uncle Rayson has been attending to his redemption himself. Now that you're here, I'm sure it will help. Once his sins are paid for and his soul is thoroughly cleansed, he'll get to go home. I'm sure of it, so try not to fear for him."

Her words are like honey. My knees tremble with the relief of it. My heart fills with joy just from knowing he's okay. I wish I could tell Ma and Pa. I know I can't. It's impossible. So as Sister Anne works the buttons free and drops the heavy fabric from my shoulders, I close my eyes as tight as I can and send the thought with all my heart, hoping they will hear. That they will find some semblance of peace.

"Alright now, Ruby. Let's get you all cleaned up," says Sister Anne, guiding me to the edge of the tub.

I hold her hands for balance as I put first one leg in, then the other. The fragrant water is the perfect temperature, and I wonder how they got it so as I slide down into it.

"There's a body sponge on the shelf, as well as whatever else you may want," says Sister Anne. "Do you need any help, or would you like me to leave you be?"

"I'm fine," I tell her, and she nods as she bends and scoops up my small pile of dirty laundry. "And Annie," I say, reverting to the name we called her all those years ago.

"Yes?" she asks, with one hand on the shiny brass doorknob.

"Thank you," I say. "Thank you for easing my mind. It means a lot."

Sister Anne smiles, a warm smile. A beautiful smile. "You're welcome. I'll be back in a while." With that, she disappears past the door and closes it behind her. Her soft-soled shoes lightly tap away, fading down the hall.

I'm left alone with my thoughts. I could use this opportunity to try and find my way to the basement stairs. To try and find Sammie. The only thing in here to cover myself with is a large linen bath sheet hanging from a hook on the far wall. I can wrap that around myself until I find something better, and I can go out and search for him, before she comes back.

Or I could wait here in this warm water. I can wash away the dirt of the day, and more hopefully the fear that still keeps a tight hold on my heart. I can let them lead me to a room, and once the night is at its darkest and the house drifts into peaceful slumber, I can slip away, into the bowels of this cruel place and find my brother. And together, Sammie and I can escape. What should I do?

*****

Wrap myself in the towel and find my way down to my brother. Turn to page 28.

I must wait. I need to do this right, or I could end up chained to a bed like Katie was. Turn to page 20.

I should listen to this voice. I'm tired and I need to get off my feet. It shouldn't take long to catch my breath.

The stair below me is soft, so comfortable, even though it shouldn't be. It should be hard and unyielding. Alarm bells go off in my head. I try to stand, but my bottom fuses to the wood and no matter how hard I struggle, I can't free myself.

The voice is laughing now. It's coming from all around, sounding excited to see me struggling.

"Why are you doing this?" I yell.

"My pets are hungry," she says. Each word comes from a different direction. "And now they will feed."

The walls of the stairwell grow up and up, forever, just as the stairs grow down and down, into eternity. It feels like I'm shrinking even though the stairs don't change size.

Over the sound of the expanding stone walls, I hear beasts coming, beasts that will devour my flesh as well as my soul. I don't know how I know that. I just do.

"They're almost here. You can hear them, can't you?" she asks through laughter. "It won't be long now. Try not to struggle. It'll be easier on you that way. Not as fun for my pets. But easier on you."

"Who are you?" I ask as the growling grows closer.

"Just another of the Chosen Daughters doomed to haunt this place. To guard its halls from all the wayward little girls who don't stay where they're supposed to." She yawns, like she's bored. As if I'm some plaything she's growing tired of.

"Please, let me go. Just let me be–"

Something grabs my neck from behind and pulls, but the stairs refuse to release me.

I slap out at whatever it is that holds me, but there's nothing to hit. My thighs scream out in pain from where the stairs have fused with my flesh.

The invisible beast behind me roars, tugging at me, tightening my skin with each yank. It burns so bad. It tightens its grip on my neck, and I feel as if my whole body is stretching like taffy.

"Oooo, you're a tough one, you are!" The voice laughs, mixing in with the beast's growling and snapping and my own shrill cries.

The beast keeps tugging until there's a wet ripping sound. It feels like liquid fire is being poured under my leg as skin rips apart. It tears slowly with every inch I'm pulled into the air.

Blood pours from my legs. The stairs are sticky with it, making my bare feet slide around, trying to find purchase.

One final tug and I fly upward. The last piece of my flesh rips free from the stair with a final *zzzip*. Blood streams down my legs and plops off my toes. The air hitting my exposed muscles is like someone blowing salt into my wounds.

The beast tightens its grip on my neck, squeezing it shut, cutting off my air. I try pounding away at the beast, but there's nothing to hit. I'm hitting myself, bruising my chin, splitting my lip, blood pouring down my face where my nails dig in, searching for the thing that's got me.

My body weight pulls me down from my neck, elongating my spine, igniting a white-hot agony. I keep flying up, the ceiling climbing with me. The higher I get, the more I struggle, and the more I struggle, the more stretched out my neck becomes.

I can't scream or breathe. My dangling body is too much weight for my neck to bear and my head aches and throbs. I'm unable to thrash about anymore. My hands fall to my sides. I've lost so much blood, I'm struggling so much for air, that my body gives up on me.

Rows of sharp teeth clamp onto my stomach and my back. Another invisible beast bites down, growling as the one above me howls in anger. As if it's mad that something else is here to steal its dinner.

The pain above my shoulders is unbearable. My neck cracks as the other beast bites through my flesh, pulling me down. All the while the voice laughs joyfully.

Strips of skin peel away from my waist. Blood courses down from my wounds. Every part of me aches and calls out for mercy as all around me grows dim.

Before I die, the one holding my neck lets go to attack the other. I can't see it happen, but rough wings slam against me, and there's the crunch of jaws snapping into hardened flesh. I collapse at the waist, my full weight held now by things I cannot see.

The other beast stops biting as it defends itself. I try to grab hold of it, to keep from falling to my death, but I'm too weak to move my arms and can't touch them anyway. The magic won't let me.

I fall fast, crashing into the hard wooden steps, shattering my feet and legs, banging my head off the boards as I tumble, tumble, tumble down.

*****

The correct answer was to keep going down the stairs.
Turn to page 36.

The hallway is too obvious. It seems like they would better hide the place they keep their prisoners. And I'm not sure I'd have made it through the wall of darkness. It seems so solid. So impenetrable.

I go right, walking toward the shadows filling up my chosen doorway. I'm mesmerized by the way the dark mist moves. It swirls and dances as if it's a living, thinking being. It pulses, and with each pulse, tiny spikes emerge and retract from circular forms. When I get close enough to it, I reach out a hand. The inner tip of one of the swirling spirals pushes out and away from all the rest, unwinding itself as it does. It moves at the same pace as my hand and when I stop, I expect it to as well. But it doesn't. It keeps drifting forward. Part of me wants to jump back, to not let it touch me, but Pa always told me the only way forward is through. I stand brave and brace myself for what will happen when that dark wisp and my fingers touch.

I expect it to be cold like the door was against my back, but it's not even cool. It has no temperature at all as its tip attaches to me. The rest of the mist spirals around my outstretched finger, continuing the same circular motion it made on the thick curtain of shadow. It doesn't hurt at all as it inks a black tattoo under my skin, wrapping around and around my finger, hand, wrist, and up my arm.

The black etchings stand out in stark contrast against my pale skin, then soften and disappear as I step forward into the opaque doorway. The swirling lines are all around me, as if the whole world is filled with them. As if they exist everywhere and not just this three-inch-thick doorway.

The shadow disappears, and the room beyond is a normal room at night. Dark and unlit, but with nothing weird or odd about it. It's just a large and fancy sitting room with light tan leather couches, overstuffed chairs, and tall wooden bookshelves filled with thick tomes.

On the wall are portraits of Father Gabriel smiling his great, white-toothed grin. The frames are all golden and brass and richly polished wood. It's a space made for men, and especially for Father Gabriel.

I look away from his painted eyes and turn back to the doorway. The swirling shadows are still gone. I'm not sure whether they had been there to mark someone's passage, or to try and scare folks from entering. But I'm through now, which I can only hope means I'm closer to finding my brother.

I look around for what's next. Another doorway to slip through, or some sign of a hidden stairwell leading to the underparts of this house.

In the middle of the left wall is another doorway. It's the only way out of here besides the windows lining the opposite wall and the doorway I came through.

I head through the door, thinking about Sammie. About he and Ma and Pa way back. About how much more devout they used to be. How much more sure they were in Father Gabriel and our extended family here.

When we were small, before Little Joe had been born, Ma and Pa made us say our prayers to Those Who Will Come every single night before tucking us in all tight. They made Sammie and I recite the hymns, and each summer during the recommittal ceremonies they'd sign us up as quick as they could to be fruit bearers. We used to hate doing it. We hated being part of the group of thirteen to carry trays of freshly picked offerings for sacrifice. Bowls of berries and ripe, red cherries next to apples and peaches and pears we'd balance on heavy wooden slabs. We'd walk them down a freshly tilled path from the gathering hall through the woods to our sacred pool. Always when the moon was at its highest, would we start to walk. And behind us, covering up the tracks our bare feet made in the soft soil, the Chosen Daughters walked after. Behind them, the Elders. And behind them, everyone else.

We'd walk until we got to where Father Gabriel stood, knee deep in the water already, the sacrifice on a stone altar rising up out of the water. Piece by piece, Father Gabriel arranged the fruit until the unlucky soul upon the altar was surrounded by it. Almost lost in the neat piles.

The summer sacrifice was always marked with fruit. Us fruit bearers stood there then, our trays empty, their contents arranged around the one whose offering would bring us either prosperity or hardship. It depended on how redeemed their soul had been made. How pure their heart had become when Uncle Rayson was through with his dark work. Our crops would either give in abundance, as would our women's wombs, or they would not.

Our trays barren in our tiny arms, all thirteen of us stood waist deep in water around the altar and waited as all who followed walked into the shallows around us. Making ring after ring until all who lived among us stood, their feet submerged, inside the sacred pool. The children too young to stand were dipped in by those who held them so that everyone was connected by the pond's water.

When everyone was gathered, we waited, the only sound the whimpering of the sacrifice raised before us. No one else made any noise. Even the babies held their cries, like they could sense the importance of the ceremony. They could feel the fear and excitement in the ones who held them and who stood around them.

It always seemed like forever before Father Gabriel broke the silence and stepped up the stones that rose like stairs beneath the water. He'd rise above the form hidden in the fruit. Those of us close enough to see swore he stood upon the water's glassy surface.

Once there, he raised his arms out wide, his pure white robes hanging as if they were the wings of some fallen angel. One hand held a long silver knife, razor-sharp and glinting in the moonlight that shone down upon us. The poor, doomed soul upon the altar would sometimes struggle, knowing what was to come, for they had once stood where many of us now did.

They wouldn't want to die, especially not for whatever sin it was they had committed. Whatever it was they had done to catch the ire of those above them. Or hadn't done. Most times it was for simple crimes. Not working hard enough in their chores after having been reprimanded. Breaking something precious while cleaning one of the Elders' rooms or houses. Saying no when they were told to do something by someone with more power than they held.

The last year Sammie and I had been young enough to be fruit bearers, it had been Auntie Jane, Ma's sister, who we watched Father Gabriel take. No one ever knew who it would be until the moment we stood there in the water waiting. Nobody knew aside from Father Gabriel that was, and Uncle Rayson.

For if we knew ahead of time who it was we were to lose, some of us may rise up against it. Some of us may try to form a plan to set them free. But seeing who it was for the first time as we ringed around them, their body surrounded by fruit we'd soon be eating, the moonlight calming us in its milky glow, we could only watch. Some of us mourned our losses silently as Father Gabriel stood there, arms spread wide. Others readied themselves to accept the ultimate gift they were about to give. But most of us just wanted it all to be over.

But the last year Sammie and I stood there in that first ring, our faces almost level with our dearest aunt, Father Gabriel's words etched themselves into my closer family's minds. Ma's and Pa's and brother's and mine. It opened our eyes the tiniest bit toward how maybe this all wasn't what we truly believed in.

"My Children, welcome! Welcome to the waters that have saved us all," Father Gabriel said, his words booming out above us. "Throughout time, we have come here, gathered 'round this same stone table, and we have asked Those Below to give us what we need to continue on in this cold and desperate world."

"Praise Them," we answered as one, as we always had and most always would.

"We give Them this precious gift of one wiped clean of all their sins. This precious being of innocence we send to Them. To live among Them as their personal servants. This is a gift to them as much as it is one for us. For they will rise again when their masters rise, when *our* masters rise, and they will walk once more among us for as long as their masters walk. We praise Them always." Father Gabriel brought his hands together, holding the knife high.

"Praise Them!" we said again, louder, for the moment was near and excitement ran through us all.

"We give this life to Them so that we may have the strength to bring Them here with us. So that we will be ready when the end is upon us to go forth into the new beginning. And They will usher us into greatness! Into the next tomorrow! Into our grand beginning!"

With those words he plunged the knife into the beating heart of our dear auntie, her eyes wide with the shock of pain. I watched as the shining of her understanding filled those hazel eyes, and I kept watching as the life they held drained away.

The blood ran from my auntie's bare chest and pooled around her, coating the bottom of the fruit like the pool covered our feet in its clear waters. Nobody said a word or made a sound. We just stood there, waiting, watching as the woman who had chased my brother and I around, laughing as she tickled us, telling us how wonderful and wise we were, died. Even Ma was silent as her only sister's blood coated every piece of fruit we had carried to her.

"Come now, children," Father Gabriel said, spreading his arms wide, the blood dripping from his dagger. "Come feast from the fruit of the fallen. Come take in her life and let us all be one with her as her soul goes on into eternity. And be not sad for our loss here today. For she will rise up with Them one day. For she will walk this world forever when she does. Even long after most of us are buried deep within its dirt." These were the words he used every year. The promises that were supposed to make us feel better as we lost another to a senseless death.

I believe there is magic in those waters, and in Father Gabriel himself, for I have felt it. But I can't believe in demons rising above the ground to guide us after the world crumbles to its knees. It's all just a way to keep us doing as the Elders wish. Scary words to keep us in line. To keep us doing what they want us to, and to keep us from running away and leaving them with nobody left to cater to their every whim. That's what their words are for. That's what their laws are meant to do.

Sammie had been given a handful of dripping berries. I received a clump of wet cherries. The blood blended so perfectly I couldn't tell how much of the stickiness was from my aunt, and how much of it was from the sweet ripe fruit. My brother ate his berries all at once. I plopped the cherries in one at a time, spitting the pits into the water one after the other. I did this without even thinking as I followed Sammie past Father Gabriel.

This was how we recommitted to him each year. To the Family. To the gods beneath our feet whom we can only see in death, or in the death of the world to come.

I wonder, as I walk into the next room, if it's Sammie who they plan on using this year. This coming celebration of death which is supposed to be a gift in hope for what's to come. And if it is true, I must find him and flee.

These thoughts fill my head as I rush into a room that's pitch-black. There are no windows, no moonlight, no way of lighting the lamps.

I keep my hands out in front of me, but my hip slams into a table. It takes all my will to keep from crying out in pain. I stand still, hoping nobody nearby heard the thud.

The silence of the sleeping house is loud, and I don't even breathe as I wait. The seconds spin out as my eyes adjust to the darkness and my heart calms. If I am caught, they'll lock me in my room, or worse, down in the dungeon.

Nobody must have heard, so I move on, rubbing my leg, which will surely bruise. I feel my way around the table and toward the faint outline of the only door I can make out through the darkness. It's one of the swinging kinds, and I suspect this room, with its long table and many high-backed chairs, must be for dining. There must be a kitchen through here. To feed the important people who eat in this luxurious place.

The door is smooth upon my palm, but there's nothing magic about it. No swirling black clouds or unnaturally cold temperature to soak into my flesh. It's just a door. A regular door to take me from one room to the next. I take a deep breath and push, worried some new, invisible magic might stop me.

I'm three steps into the kitchen before I exhale. My bare feet pad against white tile lit brightly from moonlight streaming in through windows to the right and ahead.

In the wall to my left sit two doors to choose from. Three, if you count the one that leads outside, tucked between windows. This room is filled with counters and cabinets, stoves and sinks. Butcher blocks and sharpened knives and racks with pots and pans hanging from metal hooks.

There's a noise, the first I haven't been the cause of since creeping down the stairs. My blood runs cold. Someone's at the door leading outside. About to come in.

A key is inserted into the lock while someone sings a hymn we're all taught when we're little. A song about the ancient ones who wait beneath. As their words drift through the door, I search for a place to hide or somewhere to run.

I could go back the way I came, but I hate the thought of retracing my steps. Especially when my heart tells me the way down is through one of those doors on my left.

But I'm not sure there is enough time to try them before whoever's outside enters. They might see the door closing behind me, and if I'm caught, it'll be the end. And Sammie will pay the ultimate price for it.

Closer to where I stand is an island with a butcher block atop it. Beneath it is a set of cabinet doors, but I'm not sure if there's room for me to hide inside. If not, I could drop to my knees and skirt around the outside, in hopes of staying out of sight and finding the right time to make it to the doors.

The key turns in the lock. I have to choose. Either all is lost, or I make it through to the next step. The knob twists, I hope whatever I do is right.

*****

I'm out of time and the safest choice is to go back the way I came. Turn to page 59.

Run to the closest door and pray it's the one that goes down. Turn to page 110.

Drop down and hide inside the cabinet. Turn to page 75.

There's no time to do anything else, so I drop to my knees just as the door swings open. An old woman enters, her long, white hair glowing against the shadows. I'm grateful for the darkness. Had I waited even a second to fall to the floor, she would have seen me. I could have talked my way out of it, maybe. Made up some lie about being thirsty or hungry to explain away why I'm here, but there's no guarantee she'd believe me. Even if she did, she'd make sure I was escorted back to my room, and I'd have to start this all over again.

The door closes behind her, the lock clicking as she turns the key, making sure no one can follow her in. As I listen for where she goes, I slide open the cupboard door, but it's filled with large pots.

"We prepare the bread for the coming of the lords," she sings, a song we were taught as children. "We watch it rise as They will from the heat beneath our feet. And we praise Them ev-ery daaaay." Her voice is beautiful and familiar.

I slide the cupboard door shut and recognize the woman's voice. She was the one who taught us these verses all those years ago. Her hair back then had been a flowing wave of silver mixed with gold, and her faded blue eyes were always kind. It's Auntie Ruth. Auntie Ruth who oversaw some of our earliest learning.

"Praise be to the Mother and the Father who will come, to lead us on our waaaaay," she sings.

I mouth the words as I creep around the corner of the island. There's the strike of a match and the tink of glass as she lifts the globe from one of the many lamps lining the walls. Her voice grows closer with each lamp she lights, their light flooding the room and making me ever more visible. The odds of me being caught grow and grow, and anxiety stretches its hot fingers around my quickly beating heart.

Her words have turned to gentle hums as she walks closer to my hiding spot. The urge to run toward one of the two doors becomes harder to ignore. But I'm afraid. I'm so scared of what'll happen to me and Sammie if I'm caught. Auntie Ruth makes steady progress down the wall, lighting lamp after lamp, her soft voice creating a tornado of feeling in my mind. Telling me that danger is coming ever closer, but also calming me somehow with her beautiful melody.

If I don't move, she'll see me, so it takes all I have within me to go. To crawl around another corner of the island, obscuring my view of the doors, one of which must lead down into the depths of this wretched house. This place of horror that we were brought up being told was sacred.

But now I know better. It's a place of torture. Of choices taken away. Of cruel captivity for almost all who live beneath its shingled roof.

The song stops, and my heart thumps so loud I can't hear her footsteps until she's standing above me, her hands in loose fists resting on her hips. She gives me that same look she gave all those years ago when she caught me and Katie and Sammie giggling behind the community kitchen, our hands sticky from the stolen sweet rolls.

"Now, now, now, what have we got here?" she says, her eyes dancing with the kindness she's always had, a tiny smile playing on her lips. "Is that little Ruby I see, all grown up?"

I want to say something, anything, to explain why I'm on the floor, creeping around. But what can I say, really? So I just sit back and stare up at her, my face flushed. I try to smile even though I feel like crying.

Her smile is gone as she takes in my flowy white dress. "What are you wearing there, child?"

She knows why I'm in this house. Why I'm wearing this dress, for only the Chosen Daughters wear them. A sadness creeps into her eyes. Turning her into something hard to look at because I know why she's sad for me. The same reason Ma wanted me to run when they came to collect me. Because being a Chosen Daughter is meant to look like an honor, but it's really a curse.

"Child, my sweet young child," she says, her voice soft and filled with so much regret I look up in confusion. "I'm so sorry."

"Why, Auntie Ruth?" I ask as she helps me to my shaking feet. It's not her fault. It's not her law that's placed me in this situation, for she's just as much a victim as anyone else. Aside from Father Gabriel, of course. And Uncle Rayson. "You've got nothing to be sorry for."

"But I do, I do," she says, her voice barely above a whisper. "For I'm the one who started this whole thing, you see?" She walks toward a desk built into the wall and pulls out the little stool. A sigh escapes her lips when she sits, as if she's been on her feet for hours. Then her eyes meet mine as if they're begging me to hear her. Begging me to understand. But most of all, begging me to forgive. "I'm the one who helped Sammie get that cursed phone to begin with. I had no idea it would lead to this. I had no idea that Katie would try and run, and try again and again until she made it free. I didn't see the harm in it. You young kids grow up knowing nothing of the world outside our woods and sometimes it makes me sad."

"Sad? But don't you like it here? You've lived here all your years, Auntie. You've grown old here. You've taught us the beauty in our beliefs through song."

"I used to, child, so I did. Back when I was young, when I believed in everything Father Gabriel said. And the magic is real, true enough, which is why I stay. It's why most of us do. Out of fear of that witchcraft being turned our way. But do I believe in all the nonsense about the end of things? About what's to come? Nay, child, nay. For my mother was taught the same songs I taught you. The songs her own mother passed to her and so on and so forth back for generations lost to time."

I don't know what to say, but I can tell by the desperate way her eyes pierce into mine that she wants me to say something. That she needs me to forgive her for sins that I can't find fault in. I'm glad she gave Sammie that phone, because if she hadn't, Katie would still be stuck in a room, forced to have some Elder's child that would be ripped from her arms right after it was born. And the sadness of it all becomes overwhelming. I realize, maybe for the first time this whole entire night, that if I don't make it out of here, if I don't get free, I'll be forced to have children that they'll take away from me.

The realization hits me hard. Not only will I be made to let them in my bed to plant their seed within, I'll also have to feel the child's flutters and kicks inside my growing belly. I put my hand there, above the place they want to fill, the same place I put my hand on Ma as Little Joe kicked around inside. I remember the way his feet pressed against her, pressed against me, and sorrow fills my heart.

For Ma always said how magical it was to feel that little piece of you growing inside. To know it needed you in a special way that no man would ever understand. That babes held a piece of you in them and even after they came out, no matter how loud they cried, that piece of you would always belong to them, and they would love you in a way they could never love another, and vice versa. And the thought of being made to grow that tiny piece of me inside my child only to have it stolen from my arms and given to someone else to raise as theirs, it crushes my soul. The pain of it is like a red-hot knife through my heart.

"When I found the phone lost in the laundry, I gave it to him, "continues Auntie Ruth. "Poor young Sammie, always with his questions of the world beyond our own. I gave it to him and told him all I knew of the cursed thing. The things I learned by watching Father Gabriel and Uncle Rayson and the Clerks when they didn't know I was around. For they don't see me, none of them do. I'm just the woman who collects their dirty rags and replaces them all fresh and new. And who turns down their beds and wipes away the dust from atop their shiny wooden desks. I'm no more real to them than any other piece of furniture around this place." Her words are filled with venom, and I see years of anger built up inside her aging heart. All the years of hate she's grown inside herself, waiting to be born into the world, kicking and screaming. "I stay up late to bake their bread and rise up early to cook their eggs and still they don't see me. Not really. And I'm not sure they ever have."

"Auntie Ruth," I whisper, walking to her and placing a palm against her soft and wrinkled cheek. "It's not your fault Sammie is where he is. And if it weren't for you, Katie would still be here, stuck within these walls. You're a hero, if you think about it. And I'm grateful for you, so I am."

A tear slips from one weary eye and makes its way down her pale face. She sighs, the sound reminding me of wind softly blowing through the woods outside my window in the deepest hours of the night. She places her hand over mine.

"Child, sweet child," Auntie Ruth says, patting my hand and rising to her feet. "Thank you for the gift you've given me here tonight. For the guilt was heavy on my heart and you've eased it some."

"You should feel no guilt," I say, my eyes leaving hers and looking toward the two doors. I want to ask her to pretend she hasn't seen me. To not send me back upstairs and instead let me make my way to Sammie, but I'm not sure how to form the words.

"You want to go to him, don't you? That's why I've found you here, isn't it? Your dear brother, Sammie." Auntie Ruth walks across the kitchen and opens the door on the right. She smiles and steps aside, leaving the doorway open before me. The way to Sammie.

"It's more than that, Auntie. So much more." I hurry across the room. A soft wind rushes up the stairwell leading down. It smells of dark, wet places. Rot and death and fear wash over me with that murky breeze. "I need to get him out. Get us both out. I need to get us free from here. To find our own way out in the world. Please, Auntie Ruth, please. Won't you help us?"

She looks at me and another tear falls. With it a smile blooms on her wise and beautiful face. "Your brother's cell is down the steps and to the left. His cell is third on the right. The key to his door is hanging on a hook next to the entrance. Once you set him free, put the stairwell to your back and run right down that hall. Go as fast as you can, because the magic down there will try and keep you in. Dark things happen in the under-parts of this place. Darker things than most of us will ever see." She pauses then and looks away. It's as if she doesn't want me to see the shame filling her eyes. "Eventually you'll come to a great door and beyond that door is your way to freedom. Be as quick as you can. Once you reach the surface you'll have to find your own way out. I cannot help you, for the forest is filled with beasts. Especially that way. Katie was lucky, she took the front way, out a window. You, you'll be going through the older parts of the forest. The ancient parts."

"Thank you, Auntie Ruth," I say.

She reaches out and gives my hand a final squeeze, before turning and walking toward a giant bin in the far corner. It's time for her to bake her bread, and it's time for me to take my chance.

***

I race down swollen wooden steps on my bare feet. The air grows thicker. Something about it screams at me to turn back, telling me there's nothing good down here. Nothing safe.

It's too dark to see an end to the stairwell. It seems to go on forever and ever, and with every step I take, it gets colder. My teeth chatter and white mist puffs out with each ragged breath.

"Stop where you are," a voice whispers in my ear, so low, so quick, so desperate.

I almost stumble and fall as I jerk away from the voice. I catch myself before going head over heels down and down, tumbling to whatever lays at the bottom of this ill-smelling place.

"Sit!" The voice moves to my other side this time and I jump, but keep my feet steady. It's a woman's voice. A sad voice. But speaking urgently. As if she knows something I don't. As if she wants me to hear her and heed her warning. "Before it's too late, stop where you are!"

I don't know what to do. Auntie Ruth said to hurry. That the house would try and stop me. But I haven't even made it to the bottom of the stairs yet. Who is it speaking to me in the pitch black of this horrible stairwell? Is it the dark magic of Father Gabriel? Or something else? Someone else? And if it is someone else, is she a friend or a foe?

"You'll die if you go down there." The whisper floats around me as I run. "They'll tear you apart. Rip your flesh from your bones and feast on your blood."

Those words terrify me and cause me to slow down. I'm so unsure of what to do. My eyes fight against the wall of darkness, and I pray to whatever gods are listening, whether they be above or below, that I don't fall as I run.

"They'll sink their teeth into your flesh," the voice says.

I keep my pace even though I can't see this woman, can't hear her running.

"Their tongues are hot as fire and their spit will burn like acid. It will drip into your open wounds and bubble up as it melts your bones."

"I can't stop!" I shout, though it comes out weakly. A frightened sound. A pitiful sound. But it's the only sound I can manage, for my heart pounds in my chest and my lungs threaten to give up on me.

It would be nice to take a little break, though. To sit. To rest. To think.

"You must, girl, you must," the voice says from in front of me.

"They'll suck out your eyes if you don't," she says from behind.

"They'll pull on your limbs until your skin tears and your muscles snap," the voice says, once again in front of me. "And oh, how they'll make you scream."

The air becomes even colder. Maybe I *should* stop. Maybe I *should* take a seat. Just to catch my breath a little. Just to let my heart calm a bit.

"Yes, girl, sit," the voice says softly. Gently. "Just sit."

What should I do? I'm torn. Do I continue? I've been running for what feels like forever. These steps can't go on much longer.

But what if the voice is a ghost of some past victim? What if her words are true and there are dark beasts waiting for me below, waiting to feast on my flesh and tear me apart?

*****

I must keep going. The voice is probably a trap. Something that wants to keep me from escaping. Turn to page 36.

She might be trying to help. I'll just sit long enough to catch my breath and figure this out. Turn to page 64.

"We can't take her," Sammie says. "We can't risk it. Trust me, you haven't been locked down here with her. You don't know what she's like. The evil stuff she whispers in the night. It... it's terrifying." Sammie has his hand on the door's twisted metal handle, pulling it open to leave. "Please, Ruby, listen to me."

I look back at Mad Martha. I see chaos in her eyes. It wants out.

"Let me free!" Her tone is cold.

Whatever we find outside this room might be bad, but she is certainly something we don't want to mess with. I turn and follow my brother.

"You brats! You useless disgusting little piggies. I've been denied the flesh of the young for too long. The taste they forced on me! It's not my fault I crave it! It's not my fault its absence drives me mad! I need it. And you deny it! How dare you? I *will* get out of here! I *will* be free! And when I find a way, I'll come for you, and I'll dine on all your softest parts!"

Her screams turn to wicked laughs as we slip into the hall. Sammie turns toward the stairs, to go up the way he was brought down, but as Martha's laughing turns to inhuman shrieking, I grab his wrist and pull him the other way. The way Auntie Ruth told me to go.

He stops and gives me a questioning look, but I just pull him along, putting the stairwell and Mad Martha's incoherent cries at my back. There's only one way out, no matter how much danger there is before us. And no matter how much of it we find, I know we'll make it through, as long as we're together.

***

We hurry down the hall, though Sammie leans on me quite a bit. He's dizzy from lack of food or water, and from the beatings he's taken by Uncle Rayson to redeem him of his sins. His face looks fine, but beneath his brown robe, the lowest rank you can wear, no better than the dirt beneath our feet, his body is covered in purple and blue patches and bloody strips race up and down his back. I only notice the welts and bruises when I put my arm around his shoulders and he winces.

We pass by open doors. Sammie tells me about the thin branch he'd plucked from a willow tree that Uncle Rayson used to whip him, over and over again until Sammie passed out from the pain.

Neither of us wants to look as we pass the open doorways, each of the rooms filled with horrible things. Rooms explaining the stench of death and decay. Gory sights I don't want to see, but which my eyes are drawn to. Some part of me can't look away.

Sammie sets his eyes straight ahead. "And when Uncle Rayson finally decided I could no longer be redeemed, Father Gabriel sentenced me to sacrifice. Since then I sat in that cell, waiting for Auntie Ruth to bring me down my meager meals and hoping you and Ma and Pa and Little Joe wouldn't have to pay any more for my sin."

I'm paying attention to what Sammie's saying, but I can't stop from looking in the rooms. One contains an altar surrounded by black burning candles. The light is dim, but somehow everything is lit in sharp clarity. The altar holds the long dead body of a girl not much older than I am. She wears the same gown I wear, as all the Chosen Daughters do. Her belly is forever swollen with another life tragically cut short. A promise of a future denied.

Had she been murdered? Sacrificed for some dark spell? She and the unborn babe she carries still? Her flesh slowly decaying around it as pieces of her fall away. Or had she died trying to bring the baby into this world? Had her body refused to do what it was made to do, which caused her to lose both their lives?

The worst parts about her aren't the infant she would never bear, or the tragedy of their forever slumber in this room as they crumble away to dust. Those are the saddest parts, but the *worst* parts are the places where the flesh has rotted away and dried muscle and exposed bone shine under the candlelight. The white rows of teeth set in a jaw, its remaining patches of gum slowly peeling away. The withered, blackened eyes that look like prunes resting under half-rotted lids.

Sammie peeks in the next room and shivers. "I hate dolls," he says.

Shelves and shelves line every one of its walls, and on those shelves are countless dolls. I look again and realize they are the mummified bodies of infants. Tiny ones never given the chance to grow and learn and be. Their faces stuck forever in unnatural smiles. Their lips stretched tight over toothless gums, and dried out strips of tongue poking out through fake smiles.

Their dresses are all the same, tiny white gowns to be baptized in, only some are discolored with age, yellowed and turned brittle over thin-skinned limbs. They are all in sitting positions, their arms stiff and pointed straight out in different directions. Just as real dolls sit. As we pass, it feels as if their glass eyes follow us.

I don't mention this to Sammie, who's using the wall to help him walk.

"When I heard you calling me, I thought at first it was just another trick. That it couldn't be real. I never thought I'd see any of you again, not until you saw me upon the sacrificial stone in the middle of that damned pond."

"I'd never let that happen," I say as we stumble past a room from which emanates a hissing sound. It is filled with naked bodies piled high. Bodies of the elderly, mostly. Those of us who had aged away and died. Grandmothers and grandfathers, their limbs tangled together, their skin in different levels of decomposition.

On the floor in the center of this room is a metal grate. Sprinklers rain down constantly upon the rotting corpses, spraying their cloudy eyes, running water through thinning blue hair, washing the ooze seeping from them down the drain. The smell makes us gag. Sammie quickens his step, even though it's obvious it pains him.

Poor Sammie. Always trying to be strong. To be brave.

"When I saw what you were wearing, my heart broke a little," Sammie says. "We have to make it out, Ruby. We have to."

"We will," I say, but I don't know how reassuring I sound while looking into another room where corpses are hung by their wrists and shoulders. Buckets beneath them collect black gunk that oozes from cuts around their organs. As if they were harvested and left to rot.

The next room holds an operating table, all shiny and clean and sterile. There are tools set out on metal trays and large overhead lights waiting for a body to be wheeled in.

There's a single casket in another room on our left, and whatever's inside bumps and bangs against the polished black wooden lid. Its muffled screams are of something large and angry and inhuman trying its best to break through.

The next room holds racks and racks of stretched-out skins shaped like human bodies. At the top are flattened head shapes with holes where the eyes should be, and nubs below them with long dark ovals where the nostrils go. The mouths are all stuck open, forever caught in terror-filled screams.

On and on the horrors go as we shuffle our way up the hall. Sammie looks straight ahead, as if he's already seen too much, and I can't blame him. I wish I had the strength not to look.

We make it to the end of the hall and Sammie stops, sliding his back down the wall until he hits the floor. His face flushes and dots with sweat. "I'm so tired."

"It's okay, Sammie. We got this," I tell him, trying to sound uplifting. I honestly don't feel like it's that much of a lie, because so far, so good. We made it to the end of the hall, to an opening into a large dark cave with a stone path leading us on.

"I'm not so sure about that, Ruby," Sammie says, his voice shaking, his eyes looking back down the way we came.

I squint, but don't see anything. He's just paranoid, seeing things out of fear. But just as I'm about to tell him there's nothing there, I see it too. A head pokes out of one of the doorways down the hall, and I know whose head it is.

"C'mon, Sammie. We've got to go." I help him to his feet, his eyes glued to that *thing* down there, working its way out of its room.

"How-how can it be?" he asks, his voice shaky and low.

"I don't know, but if it catches us, we'll never make it out," I say, my voice shaking and filled with urgency.

Sammie jerks his head away and we stumble toward the cave.

"She was dead, you saw her. We both saw her," Sammie says, clinging to me as we race forward, away from the pregnant corpse's shuffling feet.

"The magic here is strong," I tell him. I don't know what else to say.

I glance over my shoulder and see the mother blink, broken lids falling down over those shriveled black eyes. She jerks forward, head bobbing to one side and the other as she takes step after slow step.

The baby in her swollen stomach falls and thuds against the floor, its long, leathery umbilical cord keeping it attached to its mother. The mother continues toward us, tightening the line connecting them and dragging the baby along, its tiny dead limbs jerking with the motion. There's a raspy sound as if the baby's crying out.

The mother passes the room filled with the mummified corpses of toddlers, and one of them joins her, its yellowed dress a bright spot in the hall. Another jerks its way into the hall, its dress a dingy white. Followed by another and another. Pretty soon the hall is filled with them. Tiny shambling bodies crawling or clumsily stepping their way toward us.

"Do you think the other bodies will join them, too?" Sammie asks, his words spoken in a rush as he catches his breath.

My heart is beating too fast. I open my mouth to tell him I hope not, but before I can get the words out, a body stumbles into the hall behind the long-rotting mother. An old woman with rolls of glistening flesh hanging down her body. Two massive graying breasts swing low in front of her, and her arms reach out to us, fingers hooked into claws. Clumps of wet white hair, tinged green with algae, hang down before cloudy cataract-filled eyes.

As she steps forward, one uneven footstep after another, a second elderly body joins her. And then a third and a fourth. Suddenly they're pouring out to join the mother and the babies.

From a doorway closer to us, one of the hung bodies stumbles into the mix, cables dragging behind it. Black goo bubbles from the dead thing's mouth, seeps from its eyes, and pours from the places between its legs. It's like every organ has been liquified, blended, and boiled until it was this thick burnt goo rejected from its tired, stretched body.

Three more hanging men join the growing mass of dead things. A translucent sheet of human skin flutters from the room where they had been drying on racks.

The hall is filled with dead creatures of all shapes and sizes. Humanoid things from all those rooms we saw, and ones we'd missed. All of them dead members of our extended family. Some sewn together into things that no longer look human, things with too many arms and legs and heads. Their flesh rotten where black stitches hold them together. Others are masses of bone and muscle and white gristle clumped up and rolling forward. Unable to stand or hold their own weight, but still able to crush the smaller among them as they crunch their way along.

The sound of their footfalls is a mixture of wet and dry. A slippery sound as their naked feet slap against the floor. A raspy dry sound coming from the sandy babies, their skin flaking off with each step, creating a cloud that wisps around them.

"Why did they wait until after we got here?" Sammie asks.

I have the same question. Why wouldn't they stop us before we got close to the exit? Why wait to get between us and the only way back to the house?

Unless…

"Maybe this is a trap," I say with a shudder. "Maybe the cave leads to a dead end and we're about to be stuck in there."

"Well, there's only one way to find out," he says, dropping me a wink and the same smile he used every time he'd come to Katie and me with a mischievous plan. That same grin that would get the three of us in so much trouble. Those times that ended up being the best parts of our whole lives.

We turn away from the army of death and start toward whatever horror lies ahead. And we do it with lighter hearts because of that smile. The memories of the past giving us strength for the present.

I make it into the cave with Sammie's arm around my shoulder. He's so much lighter than he was, though I haven't had to hold him up like this before. He's lost too much weight.

We're stopped abruptly when I'm pressed into what feels like hardened air. There's the tiniest bit of give, as if we've walked into an invisible wall made of an overstuffed mattress, and we both stumble back from the force of it.

I'm barely able to keep us from falling. All the while, the monsters stumble closer. Sammie meets my panicked gaze with one of his own.

"There's nothing there!" Sammie yells, his voice filled with anger. He hobbles in front of the invisible barrier and presses his hand against it.

I can see the pressure it makes against his palm, but it makes no sense. "I don't understand," I say, pushing my hands against the nothing that stops us from moving through.

It's cold to the touch, and filled with a hum I can feel in my teeth. I push harder and harder, and it starts to give, but it hurts, as if I'm pressing into electricity. If we lean into it hard enough, it may give and let us through, but it's probably going to hurt.

And the pain from just touching it is almost too much for me to bear.

"Can you feel that?" I ask as the undead grow closer.

"Yes." Sammie jerks his hand away and shakes it like it burns. "But what else can we do? If we don't keep going, they'll reach us, and there's no way we can fight them all."

"But maybe we can," I say, trying to handle the pain in my tingling hands. "Maybe we can fight our way back and go up the stairs."

I hold my hands to the invisible wall as long as I can, but the thought of turning back to fight makes me pull them back and turn around. I take in all the beasts scuttling and plodding and ambling toward us. The amount of fighting we'd have to do seems impossible. Just as impossible as making it through the unbelievable agony of the invisible barrier.

"Ruby, there are too many. And even if we could, there's no way out through the house. Not without *him* knowing. Not since Katie made it free. Auntie Ruth told me tales of what he's done to lock it down. To keep in those he wants in, and vice versa. We'll never make it out." Sammie looks at the invisible barricade as he speaks, and then back at the approaching crowd of lurching death.

"If Auntie Ruth is still in there, baking her bread, she has a key. She can let us out," I say, even though I'm not sure it's worth the risk. "Plus, didn't you want to go upstairs when I first let you free?"

"That's a lot to ask of her," he answers. "She's already done so much. And yes, I did try and go up, but only because I didn't know there was another way. Besides, I wasn't thinking. I just wanted to get away from Mad Martha as soon as I could."

"I'm sure Auntie Ruth would help us," I say, talking fast, my anxiety rising with every second we spend arguing. "If we can only make it back to her."

What should we do? Do we try and fight our way through these horrible undead things? Or do we press ourselves into that burning wall, to where the trail should lead to freedom?

*****

Press our way through the invisible wall and hope the pain won't kill us or last too long. Turn to page 93.

Turn back and find a way through the crowd of reanimated dead to make it back to Auntie Ruth who will surely unlock the kitchen door for us, and let us flee into the night.
Turn to page 55.

The thick black shadow sealing up the way to the left must be my best chance of escape, but I hesitate to touch it. The shadow isn't a solid barrier, but a swirling mass of something I've never seen before. Like black fog condensed into the doorway, made up of a million-billion specks.

I reach out my fingers, knowing someone might find me any moment or that I'll chicken out if I just stand here. I don't bother testing it out, just rush forward, my hands held out before me. They barely break the surface before my entire mind screams at me to stop. I'm already halfway through before I realize I've made the biggest mistake of my life.

It's cold. So very cold. Like Father Gabriel's hand upon my shoulder, but a hundred times worse. I scream, and the blackness seeps into my mouth, filling it with a taste of burnt toast so dark I can hardly stand it.

I throw myself forward, needing to get through, only I don't hit the floor. My body simply floats in the thick void. It's over me, and in me, and every part of me is filled with ice. So very, very cold.

My flailing arms and legs are useless in the shadow. I swirl with it, my body breaking down, becoming more of those black dancing bits of cloud, like fog, but blackened. Now I feel as if I'm being burned, the pain is so cold it's hot.

I become part of the barrier. Part of the magic. And all around me are the thoughts of all the others who tried to pass through here, but weren't allowed.

We are one now. One. A living swirling frozen thing. We are as chilled as the dead must be, but we get no relief from the pain.

*****

Try again. Turn to page 25.

"C'mon, there's no time!" I grab Sammie and pull him forward. It's impossible to go back. I'm not sure why I considered it at all. We'd get three steps before the first monster grabbed us. There's just too many of them. And death at their hands seems far worse than being burned alive by a wall made of invisible fire.

Sammie's jerked back. He slips from my grasp. I tighten my hold, but then we both lose ground. One of the papery men made of skin twists a boneless arm around Sammie's ankle. I don't understand how it has the strength to do so without any muscles inside that empty flesh. No heart or veins to feed it. It's just an empty sack with vacant holes for eyes and ears and nose and mouth, no sound coming out as its lips grow tight with the strain of pulling Sammie.

"Just leave me and go!" Sammie shouts, his eyes shining with panic.

"I won't leave you!" I scream. I let go of Sammie to grab the papery thing, sliding my fingers into the empty O's where eyes should be and pulling in opposite directions as hard as I can. The skin-man's mouth twists into a grimace of pain as a ripping sound rends the air. Its other hand reaches for me and slaps my cheek. I bite into it without even thinking, pulling my head back to rip its face apart.

The sound it makes as the holes tear is loud and long and it seems to rile the other creatures. The babies in their white fluffy dresses screech like the sound of an auntie's nails upon a chalkboard. I want to let the skin-thing go and press my palms against my ears so I can't hear it anymore, but I can't. I'm winning and if I don't keep ripping, we'll die. It's my only chance to get us through into the cave.

"It's working, it's loosening!" Sammie shakes his leg to free his foot.

My teeth rip a chunk from the papery thing's other arm, and its eye holes give way with an even louder *rrrrrrrrrrrrrrrip*. It goes limp in my hands.

The other walking skins take pause at the sight of their defeated friend, but the other monsters press forward in a frenzy. The pregnant mother ambles faster, her outstretched arms reaching for me, the caked-up blood beneath her jagged nails a sign she must have chewed them off herself with the anxiety of being stuck here. Knowing that when her babe did come it would be torn from her breast and given to another to raise.

My eyes flick down to the little one pulled behind her, the umbilical cord taut and dragging it along, its tiny limbs flailing, as helpless now as it's always been. Just behind the mother are the naked elders with their hair dripping water and rotting bellies and swollen knees and ankles. They lock cloudy eyes on us, their broken teeth gnashing. From somewhere down the hall comes a roar so loud it turns my blood to ice. We have to go. It's time to leave this hall for good, no matter how much pain it takes to do so.

Sammie and I tighten our grips on each other and rush forward. It's hard to push ourselves into the solid electrified air. The pain is overwhelming. I scream as I dig my feet in, pushing as hard as I possibly can. Everywhere my body touches is instantly filled with fire and ice and pain, but still I press. Everything hurts, but behind us the mother and all the others come. So we scream through the agony filling our bones and we keep pressing.

Our heads and shoulders are fully in, and as the mother makes it to our backs, which are slowly sliding in, one of her jagged nails rips into my gown and scrapes my skin. The mummified toddlers reach out for Sammie's foot just as it disappears into the unseen wall, so their little crumbling hands press against it.

Sammie and I burst through the barrier. Our bodies crumble to the hard rock of the cave floor. Every one of my limbs is useless. They tingle uncontrollably, like they've fallen asleep.

The bodies of the babies pile up against the transparent electric screen, beating at it even though it seems to hurt them.

Their dried-out fists flake away with each tiny pound. The mother screams as she claws against it. Her nails are torn away as she digs into the barrier and the anger in her black and shriveled eyes bears down on us.

Horror after horror joins her at the wall, trying to make it through. They hammer their fists and claw with crooked fingers. They tear at each other to get to it, ripping away the arms and legs and faces of those before them, only for the barrier to stop them, too.

All the while Sammie and I wiggle our fingers and our toes, willing away the buzzing in our limbs. As soon as we are able, we pull ourselves up into one another's arms and run as fast as Sammie's broken body allows.

***

The path through the cave is windy and damp. Water drips from the ceiling. The rock beneath our feet is slippery, making it hard to move quickly. The walking dead still beat away at each other and the barrier. I don't know why we could make it through and they cannot, but I'm grateful for it. Perhaps it's because they're no longer of the living, and we still are. Perhaps it's to keep them from getting loose.

"I don't know how much farther I can make it," Sammie says, panting as we crest the top of a small incline, his face pale and sweaty.

"We've got to keep moving," I tell him.

"Ruby, I'm so sorry. My body hurts all over. I need to rest. I can't–" His feet slip from beneath him, and he falls to his knees with an oomph.

I place a hand on his forehead to find he's burning up. "Take it easy, brother. I got you. We'll get out of this," I say, trying to sound cheery. But I'm scared I won't be able to get him out of here. That he'll die and I'll be all alone.

"You were always the strong one," he says, laying his head on the ground and closing his eyes. "I just need a few minutes. Just a little rest."

I look around and hope he finds some respite from all this, even if just for a few short minutes. I hope I can find an escape while he rests.

It shouldn't be as bright as it is in here, but everything is all lit up. There doesn't seem to be any way for the sunlight to find us, and even if there wasn't solid stone above my head, the sun hasn't risen yet. Anyway, it's not as bright as sunlight would be. It's only lit up enough to see, closer to the light those black candles made. Bright but in a dark way. A sinister way.

It must be another form of the magic that runs through this place, put here by Father Gabriel, or something else. Something older. For the tales of the beasts that walk beneath us have been told to us since we arrived screaming into the world.

I concentrate and make out a sound from high above me. It's a high-pitched sound, like the fruit bats make at night, only louder. As if the bat in question is far larger. I scan among the stalactites and what I see refuses to register in my mind. My eyes can't make sense of it.

The ceiling is covered with bats fifty times larger than I've ever seen. They're not just bats, though. No. They're so much worse than that.

Bats are cute soft things, with fuzzy heads and silky wings and shiny, dark little eyes. These things, they're larger than Pa, and he's the tallest man I know aside from Father Gabriel. Their ears are sharp and their eyes glow red, resembling the shape of a man's.

These aren't bats. No, these are demons, waiting until they're called upon, their wings ragged, either wrapped around themselves or stretched out as far as they can go and gently flapping.

I can't believe they haven't noticed us. Haven't heard us. Or maybe they just haven't decided we're a threat. Maybe we'll be able to walk past this cavern and escape unharmed if we do it quietly enough. Quickly enough.

"Sammie," I whisper, now afraid to make any noise at all, hoping the sound of running water hides my voice. "C'mon, we have to move. We're not safe here. We have to go." Sammie stirs, but doesn't rise. I shake him a little less gently. "It's time to wake up!"

"Five more minutes," Sammie mumbles.

I pull at him, my eyes not leaving the demons. "We have to go, now!" I whisper a little too loudly.

The demon directly above us unwraps its wings and opens its eyes. The crimson orbs look down at us. I stay as still as I can, waiting to run, hoping the thing will go back to sleep and leave us be.

Sammie opens his eyes and sits up, as if it takes great effort. I press a finger against my lips and point up, directing his attention to the creatures. He jumps with fright and his hand reaches out for mine.

The demon watches as I pull Sammie to his feet. We stare back as we move our way slowly up the path. Its eyes squint down into two sinister slits, and my anxiety grows with each slow step, tightening my chest and making a hurried mess of my thoughts. The water dripping down all around us makes it worse as my heart races faster. The demon turns its head, tracking our progress.

"The path splits in two up ahead," Sammie whispers. "The left leads into a cave that's super dark. I can't see what's inside at all. And the one to the right leads down into what looks like a stream. Which way should we go?"

"Whichever we choose, we need to hurry," I say.

The demon releases its clawed feet from the outcropping and flaps its wings. It falls just enough to right himself before the flapping holds it in place, looking down now with greater interest than before.

"I don't know if I can handle the dark right now," Sammie says, hurrying as best he can. "But the stream looks more like a river, and I'm not sure I can handle a swim either."

"Why is it always up to me to decide?" I ask as the demon shrieks so loud it nearly bursts my ears.

"Because if I didn't let you choose, you'd always run crying to Pa, and he'd give you anything you wanted," Sammie says with a little chuckle.

Four other demons drop from their perches and flap toward us. Their bright red eyes stare intently at us, drool dripping from stretching fang-filled mouths.

"How can you be laughing right now?" I pull him harder up the trail. We run, a slow and clumsy jog, the best we can manage. Above us, the air fills with the fluttering of evil beasts we only ever heard stories of. Stories we only believed in the darkest hours of the night, when sleep evaded us and shadows grew across our floors.

"I may as well enjoy what little life I have left, you know?"

"Not so little if I can help it," I say, pulling him closer to the split in the path.

The cave ahead is devoid of light. I can't tell if it leads up or down. But its entrance looks too small for the demons to fit through. If we can reach it before they reach us, we can escape. But what is in there waiting for us?

And the stream really is much bigger than it seemed. A swollen canal of greenish water rushes past, roaring over stalagmites that pierce its frothy surface. If we can make it to the banks and jump in, we would be rushed away from here, away from those flying devils. But what if it pulls us under? If we can lay on our backs and float, I bet we'll be okay, and we would be able to see where we were going.

I wrap my arms around my brother and quicken my pace, ignoring his ragged breathing and his heart bump-bump-bumping as I make the choice for us. Either saving us or damning us, I'm not quite sure, but I have no time. The demons are upon us, and if we don't act fast, we'll surely die.

*****

Turn left and head for the cave. Sammie's in no condition to swim and the water is going so fast. Turn to page 7.

Floating takes less effort than running and we could both use a break right now. Plus, it's closer to the water and I don't even want to guess what we'll find here in the dark. Turn to page 35.

I pull my brother's hand, leading him down the path away from the stone altar, the path we were never allowed to follow. The side all the children whispered about, making up stories of monsters and pools of quicksand and little beasts that lived in the ferns. Some kids would find the courage to sneak this way, but would never return.

Perhaps there is some truth to those stories. After seeing the demons and the terrors in the basement, anything could be haunting these woods.

I almost took us toward the altar, toward the part of the woods we grew up running around in. But that way leads to our village. To the Big House. To Father Gabriel and Uncle Rayson.

"My kid sister likes to live life on the edge." Sammie sounds a little nervous, but he limps after me, his dirt-colored robe dripping water as we make our way across the cave floor toward the pond's edge. "You sure you wanna go this way? Risk the wrath of Ma and Pa again?"

I know he's joking, but I also know he's as afraid of this part of the forest as I am. We make it to the pond when something splashes in the water, making the same sound as what we heard in the cave. Back then, it was probably a stone falling from above, but now there's only sky.

"Let's hurry," I say.

Sammie tries to run, but stumbles over a rock. He falls and cries out.

A loud splash erupts as a giant tentacle rises up and slams down with a thunderous splat, all squishy and rubbery and wet. It looks like a long piece of purple spaghetti with pink stretchy cups on the bottom. It squelches as it works its way up the bank toward Sammie.

He lies there, staring at the massive tentacle as it inches closer. There's no head poking out of the water, but somehow it's able to come straight for him, even if just inch by creeping inch.

I rush to him and tuck my hands under his arms. He digs his heels in and pushes away just as the tentacle smacks down on the ground where his leg had been resting.

"What is that?" Sammie yells.

The thing searches for him, slapping around, as we back up. Another tentacle rises out of the pond and claps down on the moss next to the first. Then another and another. *Whack-whap-whump*, they crash down on the bank, each one inching forward, their soft rubbery ends pulling at the earth.

"We need to leave before it gets out of there," I scream over all the noise.

"Help me up. My ankle is pretty bad, but if I put my arm around you, I can probably run."

"Alright, c'mon!" I help Sammie to his feet, and he wraps his arm over my shoulders. Our run is more of a lopsided trot, but we're moving.

The tentacles pull and retract, swelling as they retreat, growing longer and thinner when they reach. Whatever body they're pulling out of water must be huge. We got to leave before it appears, but Sammie, as starved as he is, is still heavy for me. Especially with his thick dripping wet robe.

"How have we never seen this thing before?" Sammie asks.

We're both sweating, struggling to keep up this pace as the trail narrows, the trees growing closer to the pool's edge, making it hard to go fast.

"Maybe it's like the things inside the Big House, and it only comes out when people aren't supposed to be here," I say, panting. "Maybe that's why kids disappear in the woods."

A bulbous shape rises out of the middle of the pond, water cascading off it. Soon it'll be able to see us, and won't be blindly reaching anymore.

Its head is the same dark shade of purple as its limbs. Its eyes are small bright beady balls beneath heavy lids at the base of that giant squishy-looking mass. It moves its head slightly as we run, its black eyes filled with an evil, calculating intelligence.

I don't know if we'll survive a slap from one of its tentacles. I imagine a bunch of them twisting around our limbs, tightening their grips, and pulling us apart. Panic tightens my chest, and I say, "We need to go."

The thing slams its tentacles down in a wave as it pulls itself farther onshore. It's not close enough to reach us, but it will be at the pace it's coming. We need to act as fast, or we'll surely die.

Our only choices are to run straight ahead on the narrowing path, or veer off into the forest. The path will be faster, but closer to the monster's ever-nearing grasp. The forest is thick and filled with bushes and ferns. It's going to take us longer to get away, but it may be easier to escape the many-limbed creature if there are trees between us. What do we do?

*****

Stick to the trail. It's quicker and we'll be able to get away faster. Turn to page 107.

Escape through the forest. It won't be able to follow us through the thick bushes and trees. Turn to page 103.

I barely have time to decide when two tentacles crash down, one before us and one behind. I've already slowed to pull Sammie off the path into the forest. Had we continued on the path at a fast pace, the thing would have had us.

"Hurry!" I scream, crashing through the first line of trees.

"I'm going as fast as I can!"

Behind us, a great purple tentacle slides around the trunk of a large pine. The tree snaps in half and sharp chunks of wood splinter off, peppering my back and embedding tiny shards in my neck. Another tentacle slams into a tree we just passed, but this time the trunk holds as the thing drags itself closer. Its mouth must finally be out of the water, because a high-pitched screech fills the air, causing birds everywhere to take flight and call out to each other in sheer panic.

The trees grow thicker, and we slow down as we move through them. The tentacles come faster as the creature advances. It must be close to the water's edge. It slips its tentacles around trees on either side of us.

Branches scrape against us, tearing at our faces. We duck under logs and squeeze between trunks, but so does the giant monster. Fortunately, its limbs keep getting blocked by branches, and it screams again as we get further away from it.

I turn to help Sammie through a particularly tight gap between three small trees. Not far behind us, tentacles twist around the bases of two giant trunks, close to the forest floor. The trees quiver from the beast's strength. Its smooth head presses against the other side. A large and angry eye peeks through the gap, and when it sees us, the thing lets out another loud screech.

We cover our ears and backpedal as the head presses into the trunks, its purple skin oozing through the space between the pines. It's like a giant rubber balloon filled with liquid, sliding through cracks and crevices it shouldn't be able to.

The top of the head gets through, covered with scratches and scrapes from the bark and branches, dripping green ooze down its violet flesh. The bottom of its head pops free, its mouth showing a huge beak protruding from a circular hole at the base, where the tentacles join its body. Its beak is hard bone, unable to flatten or bend as it snaps open and shut, over and over.

It gives me hope the beast won't be able to follow. That razor-sharp beak is as large as my torso, and it will have a hard time fitting through the same trees we struggle through.

"We gotta keep moving," I tell Sammie. We climb over fallen trees and duck under low branches, stopping every now and again to unsnag Sammie's robe or my gown. Before we know it, the beast is just an angry sound behind us, tearing at the trees, splitting branches from trunks.

We're finally safe, though we have no idea where we're at. And we have no idea which way to go.

Just ahead, the ground slopes sharply down. The trees are still thick, but it should be easy for us to maneuver between them. However, it's impossible to tell how hard the terrain will be since the ground is covered by large ferns. We've heard of this place. From some of the children who made it back to tell their tales of almost dying in the woods. Children's stories we believed with our whole hearts, but also thought were lies.

This is the place of the gnomes.

Gnomes are tiny demons who crawled their way up from the upper parts of Hell, closest to where Hell ends and Earth begins. They thrive in spiritual places, where gods have walked and blessed or cursed. Places like where Father Gabriel brought our people generations ago and had us build our homes. Or so the stories go.

We've never seen a gnome, Sammie and I, but we heard the tales in Sunday School. The teachers always taking their time to describe what the gnomes would do to us if we ever snuck out of our rooms at night and went into the woods to find the places where the green ferns grow. The stories were meant to scare us away from exploring our borders, and mostly succeeded. But the stories inspired some of us to seek out the ferns, either by daring others or being dared. Sammie and I were dared once, but we refused. The caves by the pond were one thing, but the places where the ferns grew thick were outside our personal boundaries.

"Ruby, I'm not sure we should go this way," Sammie says, sounding like a scared little kid.

I don't blame him. I feel the same. "It's either this way, or back with Mr. Eight Arms," I remind him, even though there's not a single part of me that wants to step foot into those ferns.

"Those stories probably weren't real, right?"

"Brother, yesterday morning, waking up in my bed with the smell of Ma's biscuits filling my nose, I would've agreed," I tell him in a shaky voice. "But Today Me is much less dismissive of the stories. Today Me has a healthier understanding of the fairy tales we were fed."

"Do you think Katie made it out?" he asks. "I mean, really? After all of this?"

"I do." I look at him, my eyes fierce, boring into his. "I have to. And besides, she went out the front way."

"Ruby?" His voice still has that childish tone. "Do you think we could go around the ferns? Just in case...?"

That's the real question. If we go around the ferns it will take so much longer to get down the mountain to civilization, but we won't have to worry about the gnomes. They never leave the ferns, according to the tales. They loathe the sun.

We're running out of time. Someone is sure to have noticed one of us is gone by now. And if not, it won't be long. Soon these woods will be crawling with Elders and other brothers of the cloth, searching for us.

I look at Sammie and see my same question in his eyes. Around the ferns, or through them?

*****

We should go through the ferns because it's the fastest way down and our time is running out. Gnomes can't be real anyway, can they? Turn to page 113.

Gnomes are definitely real after everything else we've seen tonight. We're going around the ferns, no matter how much time it adds. Turn to page 108.

I don't think Sammie can traverse the many obstacles if we go off the path, so I keep us moving straight ahead. The tentacles come closer with each new slam. With each hurried step we take, the creature draws nearer. Water sprays us as tentacles crash down.

"I have a bad feeling about this," Sammie says, as a rubbery purple limb crashes down ahead of us. Another one slams the ground behind.

I bring us to a stop and think about pulling Sammie into the thick trees, but a tentacle just yanked his feet out from under him.

Sammie hits the ground hard and goes flying back toward the creature, bouncing off the dirt and skipping across the water, screaming my name.

All I can do is watch in horror as the tentacle whips Sammie right around and directly into its gaping mouth, the beak slamming shut with a burst of blood.

I fall to my knees and scream as the tentacle tosses Sammie's legs into the lake.

Two more tentacles are headed right for me, but I hold still, knowing it's no use. It's all over.

*****

The correct answer was to escape through the forest.
Turn to page 103.

We walk for what feels like hours with the ferns on our side, but they never seem to stop. The darkness blends into a growing light and soon the sun rises high into the sky and beats down on us. Our path is gone and we're forced to walk among the ferns, sweating even though we're in the shade of the thick pines.

"I don't understand. This feels impossible," Sammie says, his good nature gone. "I need a break."

"I could use one, too." I help him to the ground, where he rests against the rough bark of a pine. "It seems like they should have thinned by now. We've walked for miles."

Before I can lower myself next to him, the ferns shake and shudder. Shrewdly carved hooks connected to woven vines hurtle out of the thick vegetation and sink into us. The lines grow tight, and I'm flung face-first into the dirt. Hooks wrap around my brother's chest and arms, pulling him back against the tree.

"What's happening?" Sammie screams, pain filling his words.

"I don't know!" I'm tugged into the lush ferns. I try to pull the hooks out, but they're barbed and the lines are too tight to give me room to work them free.

"We got them!" a tiny voice calls out from a place where one of the vines disappears.

"A mighty feast we'll have!" another voice shouts from somewhere to the left.

"We'll salt the extra meat and eat for days and days!" a third voice calls.

"Praise be to the darkness!" a fourth cries. Then voices rise from everywhere, repeating the phrase: "Praise be to the darkness!"

"Ruby, I can't move!"

Sammie's hands are pulled behind the tree, hooks sticking out from his palms, vines holding him tight.

"They've got me, too! I can't get free!" I need to calm down or I'll never get out of this. But no matter how hard I try, I can't free myself. I try to stand, but the hooks pull me forward. I slide headfirst into the undergrowth, sliding into a place beneath the ferns.

I see them. The gnomes. They're real.

"Hello, dinner," says an ugly, gray-bearded, little gnome. He holds another hook. "You'll be delicious with our strawberry wine."

"No, wait! Let's talk ab–"

The gnome swings the hook into my mouth. It slides to the back of my throat. He thrusts the hook up, and the razor-sharp tip slices through my flesh and into my brain. I jerk when it enters, then again when he yanks on the line, pulling me farther along.

My fingers spasm. A thin line of blood slips from the corner of my lips. My toes grow numb. My fingers start to tingle. The hook sinks deeper into my brain, and my eyelids flutter as my eyeballs roll back. My whole body shakes as the gnomes' little hands begin their work.

I feel no pain as their knives slice in, removing pieces of me in long thin strips. They fill tiny wooden carts made from sticks with slabs of my flesh while my blood soaks the dirt. They dip their small crude hands into the blood and wipe the red across their brows like battle-hardened warriors. I'm embarrassed to admit we were easy targets.

Sammie screams, sounding a million miles away.

I die as I hear him beg for our lives. As I'm neatly cut apart. I die with the bright blue sky lost to me through the thick blanket of the ferns. I die before I'm able to be free.

*****

The correct answer was to go through the ferns.
Turn to page 113.

I run to the closest door, hoping it's the one that leads down to my brother. I know I don't have time to do anything but make it inside before this person enters the room. Before I'm caught.

I rip open the door the same time the other swings in. I dash in and close the door behind me as quickly and quietly as I can.

It's too dark to see anything, but it's not a stairway leading down. I cautiously feel around, my hands running along large glass jars used for canning and storing dry goods. I'm stuck in the pantry.

At least that leaves one door for me to choose. A door that's gotta be the right way. All I have to do is wait until the coast is clear to sneak out and head down.

In the kitchen, someone's moving around and singing. It's a woman's voice. The melody reminds me of my childhood, back in Sunday school, learning our hymns. It's a calming sound, and I take comfort in it.

I don't know how long I wait, but I grow cold. Not just a little, but shivering cold. The temperature must've been dropping slowly, but I'm just now realizing it. I wrap my arms around me, my teeth chattering so loud I hope they can't be heard by whoever it is singing in the kitchen.

"You're not supposed to be here," a female voice whispers to me, the words cold as ice. The voice sounds confused. As if she's trying to understand who I am and why I'm here.

I jump into the shelves behind me, causing the jars to jingle. I stop a gasp by pressing both my hands over my mouth. I stand there shaking, listening as hard as I can, hoping the person in the kitchen doesn't come rushing in.

"You're very, very naughty," the voice says. It's angry now and I realize whoever–whatever new thing–I've found has made up her mind about me.

"Who... who are you?" I whisper through my chattering teeth.

"Who am I?" The voice sounds confused again. As if she doesn't know the answer to this most basic question. "Who am I...?"

I can't see anything, but I sense this person in front of me. Frozen air radiates off her, and with every second it gets colder.

"I... I don't know," I say, putting out a slow and cautious hand, needing to know if she's got a body. If she's real. But the farther I reach, the more the temperature drops, until it's like reaching into a snowstorm. Icy wind blows around my fingers. "I don't know who you are."

"Who are you?" the voice asks. "You're not supposed to be here. You're not supposed to be here!"

She yells at me, blasting me with a freezing wind, forming frost on my cheeks. I try to push her away, but it's like dipping my hands in frosty whirlwinds.

"I am! I am supposed to be here," I cry, forgetting I'm trying to be quiet, trying to hide.

"Lies!" she screams. "You're all liars! All of you! I hate you, I hate it here! Who am I?" She grabs me, though she doesn't have hands, and no matter how hard I try to push her away, I can't. There's nothing for me to push against.

She slams me into the shelves. Again and again. The shelves are thick and heavy, and eventually one slam cracks my spine and my legs go numb. I only feel the weight of them as she pulls me forward and forces me back.

"Please, stop!" I cry, tears streaming down my face. "Please."

The jars on the shelves clink and wobble. From the kitchen, the singing woman screams and calls out for help. Soon people will be here, people who would seek to stop me. I wonder if it'll even matter. Another slam and my arms stop working, too.

The ghostly woman continues her assault, slamming me into the shelves. Jars crash to the floor. She screams at me as the smell of pickled vegetables and tomato sauce and soups of all kinds fill the air.

"I hate you! I hate you! Who am I? Tell me who I am!" she shouts, throwing me backwards with every word.

Outside come footsteps and men's voices. I can't tell what they're saying. Can't tell much of anything. It's so hard to pay attention. It's so hard to think now that my whole body is numb. I'm dizzy, like I'm tumbling around as she pulls me forward and thrusts me back again and again and again.

"Please," I try to beg. But my words are stuck inside my mind.

I wonder who I am. Where is this place? Who... Who... Am I?

The door is thrown open and the whole room is illuminated. The ghost is beautiful, sad, and angry. But she's also lost, and even though she's reduced me to a ragdoll, I feel for her because I see myself in her. My future. I see us all in her, the Chosen Daughters. She is the future of the unluckiest of us. Destined to live out her life, and her death, here.

I can't feel the men's hands as they jerk me from her icy grasp. I can't feel anything anymore as they lay me on the floor, their fuzzy shapes hovering above me in the brightest light. The light that keeps on getting brighter. Getting whiter. Soon it's all I see, that light. That beautiful bright light.

*****

Try again. Turn to page 74.

"Gnomes can't be real, right?" I say, trying to sound optimistic, like I believe what I'm saying.

"Yeah." Sammie nods and tears his eyes away. We stare at the path we're about to tread. "Let's get this over with, I guess."

The first step is the worst. Especially because neither of us wears shoes and anything could be hiding below the ferns. Not just gnomes, but snakes and spiders waiting to plunge their venomous fangs into us, ticks waiting to bury their tiny little heads under our skin, or razor-sharp rocks that'll slice into that extra-soft spot that doesn't really touch the ground when you walk. I shudder just thinking about it.

We walk tentatively, the ground beneath the ferns covered in soft dead leaves. It eventually seems as if nothing down there will bite or tear or slice into us. We pick up the pace, our slow walk turning into a clumsy trot, which is the best Sammie can do.

"We're almost to the bottom," Sammie says, all excited. He rushes ahead, grabbing at tree trunks to keep from falling down the steepening slope.

I follow right behind, my heart bursting with so much joy. We're going to make it. "The sun must be coming out. It's getting easier to see," I say, laughing.

"This has been the longest night, I swear," Sammie says, his laugh lifting my heart even more.

"I know, right?" I say, barely able to get the words out because I'm laughing so hard. I can't help it. I'm tired, my feet ache, and my whole body hurts, but I can't stop laughing. I'm just so happy. And by the sound of it, so is Sammie. He laughs just as hard, making it difficult for him to run. I need to stop, but I can't. The slope becomes steeper and steeper and it's all just so funny.

"Somethings wrong," Sammie says, giggling in a way I've never heard before.

"I know!" I shriek out in the middle of a laughing fit, my sides aching.

"Do you hear that?" He's absolutely mad with laughter now, about to fall, leaning with his hands crossed over his stomach.

"Yes!" I'm laughing so hard I barely hear it, but it's there.

At first, I take it to be echoes from our mad laughter, but it's coming from all around us, and from under the ferns. From where *they* are said to be. Then I know. The gnomes are real, and they have found us.

I fall to my knees, maniacal laughter forcing its way from my mouth. Even though alarm bells go off inside my mind, I can't stop, can't catch my breath. Tiny happy sounds close in on us from all around. The brightening sky grows dimmer as my vision fades. If I don't stop laughing, I'll pass out.

Sammie falls forward and slides away headfirst, his woolen robe acting like a kind of sled. His laughter fades as his body disappears down the hill. All around me the tiny laughing turns to shouts, then screams of pain as my brother crashes into a crowd of gnomes.

Their sudden alarm breaks me from their spell. I gasp for air. The ferns around me shake as tiny steps approach.

"Get her!" a shrill voice shouts from beneath the greenery.

A thousand war cries answer.

The gnomes, tiny little man-like things with pale grayish skin, noses too large for their faces, and beady black eyes, jump out at me. They run up my legs and grab my dress, using it to climb higher. They carry roughly-hammered knives with sharp-looking tips in their mouths, allowing them to ascend quickly.

I jump to my feet and spin in circles, tearing them off me. Their gray beards are stained with my blood from where they dig their sharp daggers into my belly and thighs. It's worse than getting stung by a wasp.

"She's a mad woman!" one cries as I fling him in the air.

"Kill her afore she kills all o' us!" yells another before I send him flying with a kick.

"She killed Herb!" one cries after I stomp his friend, whose knife drives deep into my sole. Five others grab my ankle and sink their tiny teeth into me.

I lose my balance and fall flat on my back before sliding down the hill like Sammie.

"Noooo!" little voices scream all around me.

"Watch out!"

"Grab her! Grab her! Don't let her go!"

All over me, they dig clawed fingers, pinch my skin, wrap themselves up in my hair. They drive tiny knives deep inside me to hold on. I scream in pain as ferns fly by, hoping to not smash into a tree while I pound away at the little creatures.

My whole body hurts and burns. One gnome makes it to my chest, standing with my nightgown wound up in his fist to keep from falling. His mouth drips with my blood, his hands stained by it. He stands triumphantly as trees race past. I grab at him, but he laughs and plunges his sword into my palm.

I scream through the pain and tighten my fingers around him. I'm so angry, I put his head into my mouth, ignoring his tiny plea for mercy, snap my teeth down, and rip off his head. His blood is sweet on my lips. I spit out the head in disgust, then I reach for gnome after gnome, ripping off tiny heads from frail shoulders, spraying blood everywhere.

The rest leap free, screaming as they do.

"She's a monster, she is!" one yells before jumping.

"Did you see what she did to Frank?" another screams as he rolls away.

"Run away, friends, before she feasts on you, as well!" one hollers before I crush him.

Just as the last one hops away, I fly off the edge of a cliff. I fall, fall, fall straight down. My back smacks icy cold water and I thrash around, trying to surface.

I can't tell which way is up. I'm so disoriented my legs tangle up in my gown. For the second time this day, I'm about to drown.

Something tugs at my head. A gnome, stuck in my hair, kicking his way to the surface. I'm grateful, even through my hatred for him. I yank him free and kick my way up. My head breaks through the surface and I gasp for air.

Sammie grabs hold of my arm and pulls me onto land.

"Hey, how about that? I got to save you, after all," he says, his voice filled with happiness.

This time our smiles and our laughter are real, not the result of some spell. The river Sammie just pulled me from runs along the edge of something I've never seen before, but I've heard about. A road. A real life actual road. All black with yellow painted lines and cars zooming, three in the time it's taken my heart to get back to normal with its bu-dum bu-dum bu-dum.

Sammie helps me to my feet, both of us bleeding from our slide down the mountain. I got the worst of it from the gnomes and their tiny little blades, but we lean against each other and limp to the hard gravelly blackness of the road.

As the sky brightens above our heads, a silver car slows down.

"Are y'all alright?" an old woman asks, concern like I've never seen before upon her face. Her hair is a mass of white curls, blowing in a soft breeze that chills me, but which can't take away my joy for seeing her here.

"We need help," I say. "We need to escape."

The look she gives me tells me all I need to know. We made it. We're finally safe. We're finally *free*.

THE END

How Did You Do?

We hope you enjoyed the book and wouldn't mind giving us a little feedback. Thank you so much for your support.

Scan below to answer a few questions about your reading experience.

Dearest Reader

Thank you once again for going on this adventure with me. I hope you have found joy in these words as well as fear. This project was so much fun to write, and I'm honored to have been given such an incredible gift as the opportunity to die with you over and over. Sharing this experience with you has been a serious highlight of my writing career and the fact that you keep coming back to read these things I write means the world to me. The whole world.

A huge thank you to Mark for making this one of the best times I've ever had while creating. His kindness knows no bounds and his writing not only complimented my own, but his words made mine better. I'm so very proud to be a part of the TNTD family and I will be forever honored to be among them.

All the love, always.

~A Housewife With A Pen

The Unfortunate End of Ashleigh H.

The ground vibrates beneath me, a low rumble I'd feel through my bones if I still had any. "It's got to be her," I say, floating off the dirt. "Please, please, please."

It's not often we get visitors, and rarely this late with the last bit of sun saying goodnight. When I first came to being, I had no idea what day it was and had zero reason to care. Not since she started coming around. Nearly every Friday night. Just her and her camera.

Funny how Fridays didn't mean a thing to me when I was alive. Not like my classmates. There was no hanging with friends or going to parties. No, Fridays you'd find me stuck in the bathroom, fixated on the miserable failure in front of me.

But that's in the past, who knows how long ago. All that matters is that she's here and I'm finally strong enough to communicate.

That's her car rounding the corner, parking in the same stall as always, smack dab in the middle.

I glide up to the passenger side knowing I've got to play this right and not scare her. She slips out of the car with her expensive-looking camera, her opened purse sitting on the seat. I don't know why she takes the photos, if it's work or pleasure, but she makes me feel special when she stops by my grave.

She leans against the hood of her car, fiddling with her camera, while I float through the passenger window and settle beside her purse. I still my mind and concentrate all my energy into my hand, sliding out her wallet and flipping it open.

I did it! I'm getting stronger and can write her a note. Her driver's license is only partially visible, but I make out the important part. Ashleigh H.

The napkin on the floor is easy to pick up and set on the seat. I slide the pen out of her purse and click it open. I've got this.

The first letter is shaky, hard to tell it's an A, but the S and H are easy to read. L is next. E—

The driver's door whips open. "Hello?" she says, her voice shaking. "Is someone here?"

"Me!" I shout even though she can't hear. I turn back to the napkin and write I and G.

She gasps, probably about to scream.

I keep going and finish the H. I need to let her know I can be her friend.

"How?" she says, reaching for the pen.

Her fingers wrap around mine in an explosion of energy, my hand flying, slamming the pen into her throat.

"No! I didn't mean to!" I scream, focusing on the pen, trying to help her dislodge it.

The pen pops out and the woman falls on her back, the blood spurting everywhere, my hands unable to stop it.

I scream. I cry.

Alone again, I watch her die.

The End

Thank you to Ashleigh Hack for allowing me to unalive her as the winner of a contest. I hate to see her go, but I'm glad she didn't put up much of a fight.

Mark Tullius

Download Your Free Copy

Includes the first two chapters and one or two death scenes from each of the first 14 books in the *Try Not to Die* series.

For More Fun-Filled Deaths

please check out the rest of the
Try Not to Die series. Available on Amazon:

Out Now:

At Grandma's House
In Brightside
In the Pandemic
In the Wizard's Tower
Wild West
At Ghostland
At Dethfest
Back at Grandma's House
On Slashtag
In a Dark Fairy Tale
At the Meadow Spire Mall
The Shadowlands
In This Damned House
In Arcranium
Escaping the Cult

In the Works:

Super High
In Brownsville
In the UK
In the Tournament of Mortem
In Area 51
In Hollow 2
In a Prison Riot
At Desperation House
In a Video Game
By Your Own Hand
Between the Worlds
In 25 Perfect Days
Hanging with the Homies
On Werewolf Island
With a TBI
With many more soon to be announced

About the Authors

Angel Van Atta

Angel Van Atta is a passionate storyteller and author of numerous captivating novels, including the acclaimed *In The Tall Trees* and its sequel, *In The Tall World* as well as her *The Children And The Gods* series. With a talent for crafting immersive worlds and compelling characters, Angel's work resonates deeply with readers, blending vivid imagination with emotional depth. Beyond writing, Angel enjoys the art of sourdough baking, exploring dynamic video games and spending quality time with her family, including her two sons and her loyal dog, Potato.

Mark Tullius

My writing covers a wide range, with fiction being my favorite to create, twenty or so titles under my belt. There are 15 titles in my interactive Try Not to Die series and 20 more in the works. I also have two nonfiction titles, both inspired by a reckless lifestyle, playing Ivy League football, and battering my brain as an unsuccessful MMA fighter and boxer. *Unlocking the Cage* is the largest sociological study of MMA fighters to date and *TBI or CTE* aims to spread awareness and hope to others that suffer with traumatic brain injury symptoms.

I live in sunny California with my wife, two kids, five cats, and one demon. Derek the Demon pops in whenever he's bored and makes special appearances on my social media.

You can also get your first set of free stories by signing up to my newsletter. This letter is only for the brave, or at least those brave enough to deal with bad dad jokes, a crude sense of humor, and loads and loads of unhappy endings.

Derek and I would love to have you join us!

For the newsletter, YouTube page, giveaways, and more go to my website.

Scan below to Visit Mark's Website

Out Now from Angel Van Atta

In The Tall Trees (Little Voices Book 1)

In The Tall World (Little Voices Book 2)

The Child (The Children And The Gods Book 1)

The House At The End Of The Lane (The Children And The Gods Book 2)

The Paintings That Hung (The Children And The Gods Book 3)

Leviathan Rising (The Children And The Gods Book 4)

The End Of Things As She Knew Them

There Was A Little Monster

There Was A Little Kitty Cat

A Mother's Choice

Anthologies and Partnerships:

The End of Things as He Knew Them

Books of Horror Indie Brawl Anthology

Screams of Sisterhood: A Horror Anthology

Screams From The Ocean Floor: A Horror Anthology

Camp Slasher Lake: Volume Three

Netipotcalypse: A Collaborative Novel

We're Still Here: An Anthology of LGBTQ+ Horror

Dead Girls & Dead Things 2 (Books of Horror presents)

The 12 Days of Christmas: A Horror Anthology

Ghost in the Machine Anthology

Unspoken: An Anthology of Poetry

Seasons of Fear: Horrors For Every Holiday

Cooks of Horror: A Ghastly Collection of Recipes

Their Fragile
Male Egos
Angel Van Atta

Brightside

Thought Thieves

Telepathy is illegal and Thought Thieves are imprisoned in a beautiful secluded town. It's Joe's 100th day and he has to escape.

The First Time

A naughty short story about Joe's first intimate encounter.

Out of the Fire

The grass always seems greener, but living beyond Brightside will be Joe's greatest challenge.

Horror

90 Short Stories

Nonfiction

MMA

Exploring the
Motivations of Fighters
100 gyms
23 states
400 interviews

Brain Health

Facing fears of
dementia from
repetitive blows to
the head.

Jiu Jitsu

Current Project
A coffee table book
featuring Mark and
his family training
around the world.

Listen to the Books

You can listen to several books in the Try Not to Die series, short horror stories , suspense novels, or nonfiction. Find your next listen at your favorite retailer or www.MarkTullius.com

Connect with Mark

Mark enjoys sharing his passions on social media. Check him out on IG at https://geni.us/TulliusIG

In addition to Instagram, you can also check him out on Tik Tok at https://geni.us/TulliusTikTok

To watch Derek the Demon, book reviews, podcast clips and more.

https://geni.us/TulliusYouTube

Connect with Try Not to Die

The TNTD series has its own social media pages.

Check them out on IG at

https://geni.us/TryNotToDieOnIG

In addition to Instagram,

you can also check them

out on TikTok at

https://geni.us/TryNotToDieOnTikTok

To watch Derek the Demon, book reviews,

podcast clips and more.

https://geni.us/TulliusYouTube

Your Free Book is Waiting

Get a free copy of this collection
Morsels of Mayhem: An Unsettling Appetizer here:
www.marktullius.com